Days of Peace

Days of Peace

RACHEL SHIHOR

TRANSLATED BY
SARA TROPPER AND ESTHER FRUMKIN

LONDON   NEW YORK   CALCUTTA

Seagull Books, 2019

© Rachel Shihor, 2019

First published in English translation by Seagull Books, 2019
English translation © Sara Tropper and Esther Frumkin, 2019

ISBN   978 0 8574 2 699 4

British Library Cataloguing-in-Publication Data
A catalogue record for this book is available from the British Library

Typeset by Seagull Books, Calcutta, India
Printed and bound by WordsWorth India, New Delhi, India

Days of Peace

PART ONE

Days of Marriage

I do not know how, but I found myself married to a man in Jerusalem. I had thought of that before. I had had a flash of prophecy. And now, when events occurred, they did so as if on their own accord.

On the other side of our wall is the flat of a secular woman. The only non-religious woman in a building that was not large, seven or eight flats, entered through a courtyard by way of a winding stone path emerging from the foot of a stairway. Every night, or perhaps only two or three times a week, women in scant clothing, their hair loose, would gather in her home, they, like her, secular. They had come to play cards. But before the game, they would sit awhile and chat, and the hostess would serve them coffee and cookies. How my heart yearned to sit among them in those few afternoon hours in which my husband left the house and went to one of the synagogues near our home,

Deborah's Tent or Nehamah's Tent, to study Torah[1] among men like himself.

This neighbour, whose name I did not know, as the inhabitants of the building used derogatory epithets when they spoke of her—in their minds the words 'secular' and 'Gentile' were derogatory—I knocked on her door that time, and she told me her name and I too was included in the familiar womanly conversation, the likes of which I heard almost nightly from the other side of my wall, when my husband was not with me, and I began to relax. Come again, come every time, the voices trailed me as I left before the game began. And I remembered that I had often heard the sound of the radio on the Sabbath from that flat through my wall, and knew that my husband would never allow it. Indeed, his face darkened when I told him of my visit with the neighbour. Unbeknownst to me, the other residents of the building had decided that she was not to be spoken with, and the sound of the radio had been in defiance of this decision or perhaps the reason for it, I do not know which. This woman is a rebel, said my husband. He spoke loudly, but did not shout. Lest she hear, I thought to myself. Let us not be the odd ones out among the inhabitants of this building, he said, and I consented. Never again did I knock at the door of the secular woman's home when my husband was out

[1] The Hebrew term for the Five Books of Moses, from the root 'to teach'. 'Studying Torah' can also refer generally to the study of any Jewish religious texts.

at his studies, and she barely responded to my faint greetings when I happened to pass her on the stairs, as if she had foreseen it all. And I remembered that her name was Helen.

How beautiful upon the mountains are the feet of him that bringeth good tidings.[2] Each morning rays of sun light my face and I am not accustomed to these as my previous flat was in perpetual darkness, whereas here the old cord for the shutters has torn and the shutters can no longer be raised and lowered. The sun floods the room with light each morning, banishing the darkness, as my husband opens the windows and lets in the cool air and distant noise. I have become an early riser. But my husband does not fix the cord for the shutter nor call in a repairman to do the job. My husband puts off little tasks and will not take care of the cord.

Two months have passed since my wedding, and I have yet to come to terms with being a married woman. My husband has given me a tiny room in the flat, containing a closet, a small rug, a low table and a couch. And at the top of the closet are carpets, rolled and neatly lined up, the likes of which I have never seen and which my husband did not roll out for me to view as he did not want to exert himself, and only confided to me his love of his carpets, as both an understanding of cultures and their histories and a sharp eye and fine taste were necessary for that love, along with

2 Isaiah 52:7, King James Bible.

other things which I knew not of, but I did not ask more, only sat on the couch, at my side a tape player into which I inserted cassettes that I had brought with me, and opened books in order to draw out questions and answers. And then, when my husband left—as he was occupied in those days with mending the worn-out collars of his shirts, and the tailor who had been widowed the year before had reopened his small workshop at the end of Palmach Street, and the way it was sunny even in those early autumn days, so my husband rolled up his shirts, seven or eight of them, and placed them in a cloth covering so he could carry them more easily under his arm on his walk to the tailor—I am at home looking about me: the flat has three rooms besides the kitchen, and hanging on the walls are an assortment of pictures, among them a nude woman reclining upon her bedding. I was surprised that my husband, who was so strict about fulfilling the commandments, could keep in his rooms a picture of a woman lying naked, even if it was but a painting, and remembered an ancient Chinese fable in a book by Shai Agnon, in which the king's architect is swallowed up by a palace he had drawn for the king. Perhaps it was fear of the king that motivated him or perhaps he reasoned that it mattered not where the palace was so long as it swallowed him once and for all. Yet I recalled a time that one of my husband's relatives came to our home—one of the Orthodox of Jerusalem—my husband being a doctor. The man recounted his ailments. My husband directed him to one of the rooms, and they both sat on a couch beneath the picture of the reclining woman, the man discussing his maladies and my husband listening, neither commenting upon the picture, and I kept silent.

There were also books in the flat, and they filled bookshelves in the bedroom and in the dining room, which my husband also called the guest room and the living room, and they looked new to me. But it was their shapes and their bindings, not their content, which were new. Some of them my husband had bought when he hastily left Sweden, which was his second home— because that was not his birthplace—to move to Jerusalem. The books were carefully bound, with gold corners, and almost identical in height and width, as though they were purchased in one place, printed by one publisher. Among them were Shakespeare's plays and books by Kafka and Herman Hesse, whom my husband cherished more than all the others, and believed that no other author or poet had ever reached Herman Hesse's rank, and that in his writing he showed everyone that it was possible to be both author and poet at the same time, and this was Herman Hesse's exceptional uniqueness. And I thought that all these books must have been purchased in a short time and under the pressure of the approaching journey to the new land, which is also my land now, to start a new life there, in the days when the large refrigerator, now standing in the kitchen, was also purchased, along with the washing machine which is run every other Wednesday, and the electric dryer which has never been used because it might be wasteful. All these bore trademarks of well-known manufacturers whose names I had heard before, and were brought to Israel in the same shipping container as the rolled-up rugs.

But even before that, before my husband had bought his new books and before he turned to the innovations of the European kitchen, and had not yet thought of the coming better days, days of rest and relaxation, full of inspiration, which awaited him in the new land, my husband's aunt set out to locate a suitable flat, and in the end she even purchased the flat in which we lived in Jerusalem. But my husband's aunt did not buy the Jerusalem flat for him, rather for her young niece, so that she could come here and heal from her ailments and the melancholy which had seized her and had yet to let her go. For her sake she had also installed double-paned windows throughout the house, such as residents of cold northern countries install in their houses, which are an antidote to attacks of cold and various kinds of noise. Jerusalem is not a cold city. Certainly not if we compare it to cities in distant northern countries, but it does have noise and the aunt was terrified lest it rouse the shadow ever drowsing in the niece's soul and banish sleep from her eyes at night. At that time, the aunt even bought books for the niece, which filled two shelves of the bookcase installed by master carpenters, whom she found one day in her rambles through Jerusalem, in a cellar between Aza and Ramban streets.

Rita, the niece—still in Sweden in those days—began learning Hebrew then. The aunt made the rounds of the three largest bookstores in Jerusalem and, with a sunny expression that never left her face, selected Dubnow's ten-volume world history of the Jews, which she chose over the six historical tomes of Graetz, whose presentation struck her as outdated. To these she added *The Hidden Light* by Buber, so that the niece would absorb something of the beauty hidden in Judaism, which the aunt believed existed, and also two volumes of commentary on books of the Torah by Nehama Leibowitz, the six-volume Even-Shoshan dictionary, Mandelkorn's Bible Concordance, the first four volumes of the *Encyclopedia of the Bible*, and a lexicon of the Bible and the Talmud. And finally, she consulted with Mr Aharon Applebaum—an incomparable book lover who ran a tiny bookstore for decades on King George Street—and he recommended Buber's *Hidden Light*, but immediately added *In the Garden of Hasidism*.—You must take it, he said, as well as the first one, even if you take it without paying. If you don't have the money, pay me later. And the aunt gazed gratefully into his eyes. It would seem that the introductory library of Jewish literature and culture was completed, and the flat was ready, at least in that regard, for the arrival of the niece who was then in Sweden diligently studying selections from *Introduction to Our Language* in easy Hebrew.

But things did not work out as planned, and my husband became the sole occupant of the flat. The sole occupant until he met me and I appealed to him and he married me and brought me to live with him in the aunt's flat after she had left this world in sorrow, after her sole niece categorically refused to move to this part of the world and stake her place in it, and informed her aunt that she felt that her illness had returned or was at least stalking her around the next corner. Therefore, it would be better not to remove herself too far from the medical centre which was a kind of home to her, where she could find refuge when her spirits were oppressed. The aunt was seventy-two years old at that time, and lived alone for three years in the Jerusalem flat, expecting the niece's arrival, hoping that perhaps she would change her mind, and expecting more amicable days which would repair the damage that the other days, the bad ones, had left behind. But the niece did not waver in her decision, and the aunt who, despite her years, looked and behaved like a woman of no more than sixty, and some even say fifty—did not manage to keep her grasp on the world because she was weak in body and her spiritual strength eroded her physical strength, and after her death the flat passed to the niece, since the aunt had previously registered the niece in the government and city records as the official owner.

During this time, my husband had begun visiting the flat so that it would not remain empty, since the aunt had passed away and the niece held her own and refused to come to Jerusalem, as he told me one evening, and Jerusalem flats should not remain empty because otherwise they shame Jerusalem publicly, as though there were houses which their owners no longer wanted and thus they remain empty. Thus my husband told me, he who was also a nephew of the same aunt, and therefore a relative of the niece, and he easily convinced her to order a change in the governmental and municipal records, which the aunt had so laboured over, so that the flat would bear my husband's name and no longer would it stand empty and annoying in Jerusalem.

The niece did indeed return to the locked and open treatment wards that were so dear to her, and had no interest in the business of flats, as I learnt sometime later, and I did not know anything of all this, while I was wandering between the rooms of the flat which had become my home and looking at the rows of new books which had never been read, and my eyes were caught by the beauty of the wineglasses and crisply pressed tablecloths lying one on top of the other in deep drawers made specially for them long ago.

* * *

On the third floor on the right lives the Eybeshutz family. Dr Israel Eybeschutz teaches at the Teacher's College, an expert on the Bible and biblical archaeology, and his wife Miriam—she edits a language spot on television and has lately joined the committee to prepare for the upcoming Jerusalem celebrations. The couple has a married daughter who always wears a long denim skirt, a son in Gush Katif, and a younger son, a high-school yeshiva student who comes home every Friday.

Every Friday afternoon, actually almost at dusk, a man's shoes are heard thundering in the stairwell. Our neighbour from the third floor, accompanied by his son and perhaps also his son-in-law, hurries by, and the father sings the songs of the synagogue, songs of the Sabbath, already floating up from him in the stairwell, and I say in my heart that he is a master of song. But sometimes it is not men's shoes that are heard, but actually riding boots, and not running but galloping and skipping two or three steps in one jump, and who could stop them. And I knew that in those days, they had visited the Western Wall in its ruins, and it stirred in its visitors feelings of yearning and rage at what is already finished and lost, and not feelings of love and reconciliation, and who could stop these people as they climbed the stairs.

Across the courtyard of the building, at some distance from a copse of slender trees bent over from the previous winter, Miriam Eybeschutz's father lived alone. In those days, the man was elderly and could scarcely walk, a widower, and when he was occasionally invited to his daughter's house for Sabbath evening meals, his place at the table remained vacant. Before these meals, my husband used to visit a pleasant flower shop on Ben Yehuda Street on the eve of the Sabbath, and would return home with an elegant bouquet in his hands, carefully wrapped and embraced by a red ribbon. My husband would lean the bouquet, just as he bought it, against the entrance wall of our flat, and would place the ends in a purple watering can, and thus it would remain until evening fell. And my husband would say, half apologetically: Miriam Eybeschutz is very strict about flowers. Because he did not bring home with him, as he usually did on Fridays, wild flowers covered with thorns from the stand at the big bus stop, but instead bought flowers for Miriam Eybeschutz at the store for rich people's flowers.

And while I am sitting with other people at Miriam and Israel Eybeschutz's table, and we are listening to the son, a yeshiva boy who is reciting his studies before his mother and father and everyone else, and I do not know if he is talking about the current week's Torah portion, and inwardly I criticize the animal sacrifices he is discussing, and the designation of the animals for sacrifices according to their types and according to the blemishes on the sheep who were not to be included in the count, and the youth was quoting, '[An animal that has] blindness, or [a] broken [bone], or [a] split [eyelid or lip], or [one that has] warts, or dry lesions'[3] and all those would not be counted, and then I see that the father's hands holding the prayer book

3 Leviticus 22:22, translation from the site www.chabad.org (http://www.chabad.org/library/bible_cdo/aid/9923/jewish/-Chapter-22.htm)

are trembling, lest his son stumble in his words, and I regret that I found fault with him, thinking that he was dealing with minor things that had no importance or goodness or beauty, and gloom overtakes me. And I recall the days when I so loved to think about my husband and imagine his appearance from a distance until nothing else mattered to me, even if I was walking endlessly in the burning sun or someone had cut in front of me in line for stamps at the post office or some rude person had pushed me or I couldn't fall asleep for love, and a lump in my throat threatens to burst out into the world or stay inside me for ever.

The married daughter lifted her baby before all the guests at the table: say goodbye, Simi, you're going to sleep. Sha–bat sha–lom,[4] she says with slack diction. And the baby, in clothes too big for her, is not happy. She has stayed here long enough. She has already seen everything and taken in everything she can, and she does not want any more. She has had enough. The infant.

* * *

But the Eybeschutz family did not invite us to dine with them every Sabbath eve. We did not always hear the youth's pleading voice: '*Our sages taught: When do we bless the candles? The House of Shmaya says: In the evening, when the stars come out, and those who are strict go down to the river to immerse themselves*'. . . and the father's hands

4 'A peaceful Sabbath'.

tremble . . . Most Sabbath evenings we are on our own. Before nightfall, in the local store, my husband buys all kinds of food for the Sabbath evening meal and the next day's midday meal, and is strict with me to make sure that I do not light the Sabbath candles after the Sabbath has already begun, and he even arranges the candlesticks on the table before nightfall lest I move them accidentally, given that they are among the ritual objects which one is forbidden to touch on the Sabbath. And on Saturday nights, at the close of the Sabbath, he would light the thick candle and say the blessing and sniff the fragrant spices and then come without a word and seat me on a chair at the table, and enfold my body with both his arms, murmuring: a good week, a good and blessed week. But the Sabbaths were tedious.

It was hot in Jerusalem at that time of year. Sometimes we would set out on a walk towards Rachel Imenu Street and the German Colony. There we passed a building of small hewn stones built by an architect who had made a name for himself at that time and had become world famous. But when the construction was finished and the house stood on its own, it seemed to the man who had commissioned it—proprietor of the Romano chain of jewellery stores throughout Israel and Europe—that the house did not stand on its own at all. That is, it stood on its own, but not facing in the right direction and not 'as per agreement in the original contract', that in fact, the front door and porch leading up to it were facing south, when they were supposed to face east 'as per agreement'. From the time Mr Romano discovered the error, his soul was distressed, and he could not find rest. At that time, he was busy developing artificial gold nets which would be no thicker than a common spider's web, but would be five hundred times stronger and would be used for bracelets and brooches on which gems would be mounted. And here, even thoughts of his invention, which had been so dear to him up to that day, no longer held his interest (and it was his sole pleasure then), and he just continued to pretend to his colleagues, store owners like him and heads of agencies throughout the world, that development of the gold webs was progressing and raising interest among suppliers in China and Russia, but in fact it was not so. Mr Romano knew that until he solved the issue of the house he would not find peace of mind and that without tranquillity and the enthusiasm that tranquillity allows, no success in the jewellery business would be forthcoming, and therefore it would be better to hurry and sell his property before evil rumours began to spread in the market. And how did the matter end, I asked my husband. It ended well. A delegation of engineers was brought from Poland, who laboured to move the house from its erroneous location, five centimetres at a time, until the house was once more as it had been originally envisioned by its designer. And who is the designer, I asked? He who first imagined the house, or he who drew the maps and supervised the work to make sure it was done properly, even if it did not come out well?—This work took two years, my husband answered, and I did not find an answer to my question in his words.

From the house with the hewn stones we continued towards one of the public parks carefully tended in the city, after the war that destroyed the country's borders, to lend it the look of a peaceful international city. Dry and hot were those Sabbath days, and even if the heat was barely noticeable when we left the house, it became more and more difficult the longer we walked, until we became two people in search of shade who met each other by chance on the way. It comes to me that my husband then wore a coat slightly frayed at the collar. Perhaps from this something was created at the very beginning. Something in me changed towards him. We ordered coffee and cake and these were spread out on the small table, and my husband burst out: Don't touch the whipped cream. And I already knew then that he was a doctor, and I thought: Someone is taking care of me. And afterwards: Wednesdays will be our days ... and afterwards, after some reflection: When is the cleaning woman coming ... When will the class on Maimonides begin ... When do they finish the classes at the synagogue and begin singing ... And he and I inhabited different cities then ... And more: A Jew must say three prayers every day, and that does not include the prayer before sleep: the morning prayer, the afternoon prayer, and the evening prayer, and among these only the morning and evening prayers are important.

Not that the afternoon prayer is not important, but one can say it individually because it does not require a quorum of ten men in order to say it, thus my husband explains to me, and suddenly he jumps from his seat and heads towards one of the corridors of the shopping centre. In a short while he returns with a joyful expression: There, you see, I prayed the afternoon prayer. To pray the afternoon prayer, a man is not required to change his custom and arrange his day specially. And I learnt these things like a child standing before the display window of a toy store, and within it all sorts of model aeroplanes and ships, and a globe that lights up by itself with a yellow light and spins until the light goes out. And the child learns everything with his eyes.

And in the parks not all the benches are in the shade. And, of course, those not in the shade are the ones that are vacant, because other strollers, like us, are thirsty for Jerusalem's shade. And we sat by the entrance to the park, not in the park itself, because the nearby street had the additional shade of empty bus stops and sheltering roofs for sale since the previous day with no buyers. At that time, an Arab woman from a village bordering Jerusalem sat next to my husband.—Sir, money for the home, money for the children, she addressed him. And my husband frowned: Sabbath!! Sabbath!! he cried angrily, because he did not carry any bills or coins on him on the Sabbath. And the Arab woman did not accept these words of explanation, and did not speak Hebrew well and also did not know the Jews' customs, did not know that they would not carry money on the Sabbath, or even touch it, and just sat in her place on the bench next to my husband, lest he reconsider, because she had not given up hope of this gentleman. And my husband continued to yell at her: Sabbath! Sabbath! And since she did not say anything and just continued to sit there, he said: Go away, get out of here! And he punctuated his words with gestures. And to myself I translated his words into Arabic, 'ruch min huna', but did not utter these words aloud, and the Arab woman did not budge from her place because she was tired like us.

After all this, we returned to the park trailing a group of Russian speakers. The afternoon hours were waning and a shadow rose over the park from the west, close to the sandbox, and next to it mingled Hebrew, Russian, and the formless language of babies, which is a jumble of all the languages in the world. A Russian grandmother joined us, clutching plastic bags, and she squinted to see into the distance. She was forever seeking the image of her grandson, and this young man was climbing up iron steps to the back of a blue elephant. My husband took out a wrapped coffee candy from the pocket of his trousers. You won't catch cold? he said to the grandmother sitting next to him at the park, for dusk was already falling, and a dry, strange chill was approaching us from the direction of Mishkenot She'ananim.—You'll catch cold, you should button up your sweater, he said to the grandmother and popped a coffee candy into his mouth. He is a doctor, and familiar with human foibles. But a person is free to follow the whims of his soul, I said to myself, and my husband turned to me saying: Tomorrow we are invited to Professor and Mrs Yakov's.

At Professor Yakov's

Professor Yakov and his wife live in one of the old flats on Haportzim Street. Almost his entire adult life, Professor Yakov has been in the service of the Biblical Archaeology Department of Hebrew University, first as a teaching assistant and ultimately as a full tenured professor, and now as a full tenured professor but emeritus. And his children, who started out as demanding infants who would not let him devote himself properly to his work, grew and became, themselves, first parents and then grandparents to their own grandchildren. Thus Professor Yakov is an old man. He lives on the second floor of an old building of Jerusalem stone, and he viewed my husband merely as one of the regulars at the Ohel Deborah synagogue, until he heard that he was a doctor, at which point he took a special interest in him.

Professor Yakov's wife is also named Deborah, but that is not the only reason for the couple's long-lasting marriage, and their small circle views them as a model of stability and true love. When we come in, they greet us coolly, in the way of Jerusalemites who extend a limp hand to say 'hello' and at the same time check the guest's reaction. And perhaps, to be more precise, they greet me coolly, while welcoming my husband gladly, as if to say: You, who are one of us, and we value your merits highly, what were you thinking to marry a lesser woman?

We take our seats. They serve us grapes and glasses of water, like tight-fisted Jerusalemites. But Deborah Yakov talks about her ailments. Ohel Deborah is not suited for praying in, she says, it's not heated at all. And when winter comes, one can't take off one's coat during prayers for fear of catching cold. But who can sit with a coat on and turn the pages of the prayer book? And also there is nothing to dry up the mildew, she adds. And in the summer? I ask.—There is one air conditioner, Deborah answers briefly. I understand that the air conditioner is the main cause of her ailments, since Deborah's seat in the synagogue is in its shadow and nothing can be done to change the situation. But Professor Yakov and my husband delve into a different conversation. My husband expounds on his ongoing troubles before his wedding, at the Swedish consulate in Israel.—And it got all the way to the Chief Rabbis, my husband adds, because my certificate of bachelor status was not considered valid by Jewish law, since Swedish residents are not strict in such matters, whereas here people are strict, even extremely so. And when it was found that my certificate of bachelor status was invalid by Israeli law, it even turned out that I could not get married at all, and the two sail away on their words. Professor Yakov offers to help . . . He has connections with the authorities . . . —But we are already married! my husband cries, and I detect a note of grief trembling in his voice. Indeed my husband's voice is no longer as it had been before.

Things are always changing in the world, I say to myself, and I close my eyes for a moment. Some kind of conversation is taking place in the room. Not in full swing and not slack. It is in a monotone. When I open my eyes, I see Professor Yakov peeling himself an apple in narrow strips and holding them up to the light like snake charmers of past generations. Not everything depends on us, I thought to myself, closing my eyes is entirely in my power, it is completely mine. Indeed, a person is actually given quite a lot of freedom, to close his eyes. And not necessarily forever. And between these two, opening one's eyes—a delivery room with pink tiles and a round clock showing the time, forever 2.40, and a delivery room like a big bathroom, it is also forever—and closing one's eyes forever, here is a marvel: this does not depend on us. And Professor Yakov is still speaking.

What does Professor Yakov say? Since time immemorial he has been organizing a project in his head; the world has never seen anything like it.—Here, we possess the Bible, and it is ours, it has always been ours and in our possession, one could say . . . because part of it was written by divine hand and part by human hand, but this part too ... up close you can see it ... and I am listening: Soon God's answer to Job will arrive. From the eye of the storm it will arise with thunder and a great silence found in all this. Wonders await us. New daughters will be born to Job and the livestock will also return and be healed. And my eyes are wide open, even though I very much want to sleep. I want to sleep but there is no bed. I think about the phrase they would say to me when I was still a young child and they lifted a chicken over my head in the ancient Kapparot ritual before the Day of Atonement:[5] 'This chicken goes to its death and we go to a long, happy life.' They said 'death' but I heard 'bed'.

Twenty-three thousand verses Professor Yakov counted in all the books of the Bible. He counted them using a computer he bought for himself, since he did not rely on the Gentiles' count, and he came up with twenty-three thousand verses and another one hundred and eleven verses in the overall total, though he did not include these in the count. And he calculated to himself how to divide all these among two hundred and thirty people, men and women and even youths of tender years or elders in institutions. He wanted to put together a handsome presentation, from all over the

5 An ancient ritual before the Day of Atonement in which a Jew lifts a chicken over his or her head, reciting: 'As this chicken goes to its death, may we go to a long, happy life.' The chicken is then slaughtered and given to the poor.

world. Each person would copy one hundred verses in pure, beautiful handwriting, while he, Professor Yakov, took on the job of copying the one hundred and eleven remaining verses. Each one should write them on paper of the highest quality, of which Professor Yakov had discovered the secret of its manufacture when he was not yet a professor and was not more than thirty years old, he had recently married Deborah, and his oldest daughter Carmela had just been born, and the reams of paper were stored in the museum of the archaeological treasures of the university where Professor Yakov was among the young teachers, and they lie there to this day, five decades later, under constant temperature and comfortable conditions, but the writing was never completed. For those many days had passed almost unnoticed, and Professor Yakov had been busy most of this time preparing his lectures and promoting his own issues with lecturers who had other interests, and the verses were somewhat neglected. Neglected but not forgotten, for with his guests Professor Yakov would bring up the story of how it all happened. And in the end, so he said, he had found himself nine copiers from among the 'faithful Christians' in a South American country but these were not enough, Christians were not enough . . .

* * *

The sky is burning hot. We are still wending our way. Where to? Perhaps to one of the parks. To stroll. A man must, must take it upon himself. My husband's face is expressionless. A patrician nose. Here he pretends to smile. Slightly dark skin, like the ancient Semitic peoples. What was he thinking when he married me . . . That we would listen to music together . . . On weekdays we would listen to music. And indeed we once heard the Fifth Symphony conducted by Bruno Walter. My husband has great respect for the conductor Bruno Walter. And just then his friend from Hadera called on the phone. He wanted to ask about his illness, because cancer had attached itself to his body and he did not know what to do. And my husband, as a wise expert, advised him. He should follow the doctors' advice. And what do the doctors advise? Rays, my husband said, because he did not speak Hebrew well. Rays or hormones, they come down to the same thing. But with hormones—they will make you grow breasts, and with rays—there are no damaging side effects, but you do what you think best. And now, my wife and I are listening to music together, my husband said happily.

We listened to music, one time we listened to music. And once we read a story that my husband opened before me, called 'The Garment', and it is a sort of allegory about man and God, but truthfully, about a man and his wife and about a wife and her husband who like each other without speaking of it, and if they were to say it—they would not be able to stand each other. We also opened the first chapter of the Mishna, Tractate Eruvin, and read, 'The House of Shammai and the House of Hillel did not disagree concerning an alley that was less than four cubits [in width], that it [may be validated] by either a side-post or a crossbeam. About what did they disagree? In the case of one that was wider than four, and narrower than ten cubits: The House of Shammai says: both a side-post and a cross-beam [are required] and the House of Hillel says: either a side-post or a crossbeam'[6] . . . And my husband reads out loud just as he sings the Sabbath songs from the prayer book on Friday nights. And I, as an architect, do not understand where the words are leading, and what differentiates a side-post from a crossbeam in the alley under discussion, and my husband continues in the same melody to himself: 'Side-posts may be made of anything, even of an animate object, but R. Meir forbids this. It also causes defilement as the covering of a tomb, but R. Meir ruled that it was not subject to defilement. Women's letters of divorce too may be written on it, but R. Yossi the Galilean declared it to be unfit'[7] . . . And I hear the words 'letters of divorce' and a cold shudder runs through my body.

And only on the Sabbaths we would wander again, and once we got all the way to the Beit Hanatziv promenade, and retracing our steps, came to the park where we had visited in the past, but this time we approached the park from the east and we just passed by the bench where once my husband sat next to an Arab woman

6 Mishnah Eruvin, Chapter 1, Mishna 5. Translation taken from: http://bit.ly/2m5Y66d.

7 Ibid.

and yelled at her: Sabbath!! Sabbath!! And we did not sit on it even though it was shady at that hour and all the other benches were in the sun. We reached the Cinematheque building, silent and almost without passers-by because it was the Sabbath and only the adjoining cafe was open and the waiters' silhouettes could be seen from afar. And I wanted to say: I feel suddenly very weary. Perhaps we'll have some coffee and I will feel better? And I sat myself down, and my husband left. I remembered stories I had read in a book, and also Professor Yakov's story, for that man reserved all his love solely for his wife Deborah his whole adult life, and put off his other love for the project of copying the holy writing, that he planned for all his adult days until he abandoned it irretrievably because his days on this earth became few. I recalled Professor Yakov's life story and thought: What will I say to the waitress if she comes to ask me what I want? For I am a married woman, and it is not my husband's way for his wife to buy something with money on the Sabbath, even strong coffee in a moment of weariness, while he continues to wander through the world without a penny in his pocket, and I let the coffee be.

I left the Cinematheque building, and the skies were still blazing blue. I thought to myself, Perhaps I will find my husband in Liberty Bell Garden. I set out on my way and crossed a field blooming with blue flowers. I wondered to myself what these flowers were called, that are beautiful to behold and give forth a darkly sweet fragrance, and I could not remember. I trod a goat path on which not even a goat had passed, and I reached its end where it joined the park fence. And in the park, again, Russian women, grandmothers, sun, straying babies. And I did not see the Arab woman again. Next to the slide which was the blue elephant's trunk, I looked for my husband. But chance did not favour me, and my husband was not hiding from me among the babies. And I was seeking to prevent a fight. I was sick and tired of anger. I looked around me, as one does in parks, and could not find a bench in the shade, and I turned and found myself a place at the edge of the park. I stretched out on the green grass under the trees. Not far from me, a boy sat down next to his mother who was lying there. He appeared to be about fifteen years old, and the two of them began discussing the boy's art, for the boy was a pianist who took lessons with a teacher in Jerusalem. They spoke quietly, and from their words I learnt that they were waiting for the arrival of a certain Mrs Klotild, a world-renowned piano teacher, who was about to arrive in Israel. And then she will hear you, my son, my boy . . . the mother says, and perhaps only in my thoughts did she say those words, as my mind clouded over and I sunk into sleep.

When I awoke there was no one next to me, for the mother and son had left the grass and it was almost dusk. I was alone in the park and no straying babies' voices were heard, and no one could be seen. And I did not seek my husband's image any more, and I said to myself: I will go back to the flat where I live with my husband, and still I followed the path that he usually took, and crossed the avenue of cypress trees as a sort of shortcut home, and from the top of the hill, on the side with the old leper colony, I saw again the building being raised in honour of the Institute for Progressive Judaism, headed by Professor Yedidyah Shalom who came from the Diaspora to settle with us, and here he spreads his teachings and lectures on the modern character of earliest Judaism, and the construction progresses noticeably every day. And the building gets taller and taller. And I rested a little in the courtyard of the old leper colony from which a certain dimness spread and welcomed me in its own way. Fruit trees were jumbled together with other trees and the ground was not grass but, rather, battered soil. It was dark, like earth that sometimes is drenched and other times hardens to a dry crust, and thus for countless generations, with no direct sunlight, and wars and famine pass over it without causing any real harm because the agents of these disasters are afraid of the old leper colony on account of its name, and detour around it, and only the disease does not recoil from it because it does not recoil from anything in the world. And the guard of the leper colony still retained some of his good looks, because he had been a handsome man before the disease struck him while he was in Algeria, a mercenary soldier fighting for the French in the Middle East, and his battalion which was sent to Lebanon stayed some time in Jerusalem as a reward for outstanding military service, and somehow it was in

Jerusalem that the guard was struck with his disease, he who was not yet the guard of the leper colony but a soldier in the army of the Republic, and he bore his leprosy secretly and unconsciously until then. The battalion therefore continued on to Lebanon and the guard remained behind in the leper colony from then on. But unlike the other residents of this building, the guard recovered from his illness, and moved to a dwelling built for him next to the building and outside its thick walls but still within the wall enclosing the courtyard, and since then he has cared for the courtyard grounds, working the soil and watching over it, and he sees this as his main function, and thus he fulfils the expectations of those who first hired him, a long time ago when he still lived in this building, that although a disease had roosted in them and even ate away at them every day, is it not like that always and everywhere? the guard asks as he tells me these things while I am lingering there. But I was healed, he said, and since I recovered I have not got sick again, not even for a single day, no need to be afraid of me, madam. The guard placed one hand on the trunk of a loquat tree and the other rested on the back of the bench where I sat. And all the people who lived here and filled up this place with requests addressed to me—because even back when they stayed here I was the guard and all their requests were addressed to me—disappeared or changed. Either because of their advanced age or the ravages of the disease which would eventually have its way with them, and my employers, who signed a new employment contract with me each year, so that they would not be responsible for my future fate—they also left this world one after another, and also the director, Sir Montefiore the Elder, passed away—and I thought that elderly gentleman would never die . . .

The heat of the day had already passed by this time. Your words are strange, I told the guard, and who can guarantee that you speak the truth? And since they are no longer employing you and no longer firing you, what do you live on? The truth is that the guard's hand was still as white as snow. I let him go. I said to myself: I will not ask anything else, not even about the professor and the nurse who lived here together in perfect love. He has had enough with all the questions people have heaped on him up to now.

Goodbye, I am going now—I bleated. Please come back and visit, the guard said, I don't have anyone else who will come besides you.

* * *

I did not have much farther to go. The afternoon hours had passed, houses that I happened upon along the way bore narrow signs, on which were written from top to bottom: *The People with the Golan Heights*,[8] passing cars were covered with signs, bearing dust from the desert—*Hebron Now and Forever*—*The City of the Patriarchs is the City of the Children*—and where was I all

8 The slogan of a campaign to annex the Golan Heights, then part of Syria, to Israel.

this time? Here I had become distracted from reality for a few moments, and reality had changed so much. I returned to the flat. This time I could not find the key that I always carry with me. I knocked on the door and my husband opened it. Where have you been wandering off to? he asked with a welcoming smile.

At the Johaness Family

The Johaness family, a man and his wife, live on the floor below us. If our floor is considered the middle floor, the floor on which Mr and Mrs Johaness live is called the lower floor, even though there are likely to be floors below them such as those known as the ground floor and the basement. Mr and Mrs Johaness are not young and perhaps because of this, they show real concern, if not actual fear, for their health. And they have an additional reason for concern, for from the first day I saw them, Mr Johaness was blind and his wife assisted him with almost everything. There, in the courtyard, where I first saw them, Mr Johaness leant over to his wife and kissed her. I did not yet know how rare was such an expression of gratitude.

At that time, they invited us to lunch at their house. Perhaps they wanted to evaluate me, or perhaps say to my husband: Here, you are a friend to us, and whatever you choose—we are with you, even if you make a bad choice. We sit at the table and Mr Johaness' wife serves hot noodle soup. Only the clink of spoons can be heard, and then—faint swallowing sounds. Mr Johaness' wife watches over her husband to make sure that the soup does not drip on the tablecloth on its way to his mouth, because in our honour she has taken out a clean, ironed tablecloth from the closet. And Mr Johaness brings the spoon to his mouth properly and says: This soup is not good. And eats it anyway. And later says: Hot soup on a hot summer day—not good. But Mrs Johaness is not deterred and does not say a word, as though she is used to suffering two criticisms for every one of her actions, and only to my husband did she complain, when she met him by chance in the courtyard or on one of the benches that the Jerusalem municipality installed for its citizens on shady street corners, that her husband's constant demands would be the death of her, and that she had to take a trip somewhere and rest a little. To recharge, she said, at home in France she left her daughter who remained there after they themselves left and came to Jerusalem, and she has two children. But when I sipped the soup, I did not know all this and just sensed that Mr Johaness' face was stony, and that his wife's was equally stony.

But Mr Johaness was not always blind. When the couple decided to cut their ties with France and settle in Israel, and in Jerusalem of all places, Mr Johaness was still healthy in body, but in Jerusalem of all places the disease burst upon him cruelly and perhaps he was the one who did not know how to protect himself from it. Although they did not give up their French citizenship, and now held dual citizenship under our country's law which permits its citizens to hold foreign citizenship at the same time, what good is French citizenship now to Mr Johaness and his wife, with all its wonderful medical services, which the couple were wont to praise to their new acquaintances in Israel, who would get up early and rush to grab a place in line for the laboratory at the General Health Fund clinic, while blindness, even if it comes on gradually, does not recognize national borders nor differences in health-care systems, and they are all the same before it?

In France, Mr Johaness was part owner of a small printing house which specialized in printing advertising flyers, wedding invitations and business cards. Occasionally, it also produced schoolbooks for elementary-school children, bereavement notices and invitations to memorial services. Business thrived. The senior labourers (one of them was customarily apathetic) were aided by two teenaged girl apprentices who helped out with the simpler tasks, while Mr Johaness spent most of the morning hours sitting in the little corner office he had set up for himself in the gallery above the printing area and beyond the clatter of the presses, which nevertheless invaded the room unhindered.

Mr Johaness brought a meal from home every day, usually a sandwich of spicy goose sausage. Since he observed the Jewish dietary laws, he carefully avoided visiting the workers' kitchens and kiosks that had sprung up in the small industrial area and served the hundreds of labourers and managers who worked there. He would finish off his meal with a cup of tea prepared by an apprentice to a senior press operator, and every day at midmorning, about eleven o'clock, she would knock on the perpetually open door of the tiny gallery office and ask: Mr Johaness, can I offer you a cup of tea or something cold? And he would always respond: A cup of tea . . . as long as you are offering. He was pleasant to other people before he became blind, and he enjoyed hot beverages. Those hours while he was finishing his meal and sipping his tea, he would turn to straightening up his desk, primarily sorting the special business cards which he particularly liked, all products of his presses. First, he would study one card which gave him more pleasure than all the rest, one rather unique, which he kept because of its strangeness. He read: *Yohanan Salomon. MA—Historian. Researcher. Graduate in Political Science (MA in History); Secretary Type 2; Shorthand; General Advisor.* At first, reading this card would draw a brief burst of laughter from Mr Johaness. As the years passed, he could recite the text by heart with his eyes closed, holding the card in the palm of his hand, and even then he would smile to himself. But sometimes the smile would be tinged with sadness, for he felt sorry for that young researcher (who in Mr Johaness' imagination had already become an ageing researcher and then an elderly researcher) whose life circumstances had caused him to abandon his initial hopes little by little (and Mr Johaness discerned clear stages in the fall from a state of limitless ambition to some kind of effort to recover from it, to conquer disappointments and setbacks and make compromises) and replace those hopes with new, more modest ones. Just to find a job of some kind, Mr Johaness would say to himself, and move on to the next card. Like a theatregoer he was, and perhaps like a writer, before he became blind. And after that he remembered what was written on the selected cards that he had kept in a small, straight-sided wooden box which he placed, carefully packed, in his suitcase before the journey. And in Jerusalem, too, he would muse on the treasure in the box. Indeed, it was not exactly the same thing. For in Jerusalem he was blind, and the printing presses that his daughter had long ago sold, after a failed attempt to revive them, and with them the gallery, and the precious morning hours and the little clerk offering whatever drink he liked and him saying, A cup of tea . . . as long as you're offering— all these things are gone. The gallery and the printing presses, the door eternally open, the smell of grease from the inner wheels of the presses and the face of the day labourer, the apathetic worker whom Mr Johaness had hired long ago and never regretted it, and the metal railing painted green winding up to his room and the sun setting in the dusty window, and the face of his wife Henrietta also disappeared together with the world.

And the business cards—how could he not remember?

Here—Golda Liddlehart. Age 46. Divorced. Seeks suitable partner.—Of course.

—Expert metalworker. Repairs made at the client's home.—Of course.

—Heavenly Dream Upholsterers. Yehuda and Arieh Levi. Upholstery work for the young at heart. Holon.

—Zelda. Seamstress. Repairs. (Socks too). Kira'on. Commercial Centre.

—Tzili Regev. Nail renewal and polish repair. Kfar Rupin College. Mobile Post 7, Galil and the Valleys.

—Mira Weissgal. Illustrious teacher from Moscow. Ballet for girls! Details available next to Bethlehem Square, Jerusalem (ask at the tailor's).

—Clowns!!!! For birthdays. Also medical clowns. Immobile clowns (also, Arab medical clown). See: Centre for Supplying Clowns and Body Paint for Events. 12 Bar Kochva St, next to Dizengoff Square. Tel Aviv.

—Languages!!! How do you learn two or more languages at the same time? Ages 7 to 70. Special method. A guy from Latvia!! Andrei Spivak. Manhattan Gallery. 12 Florentine St.

—Yargazi External School. Prepare for matriculation exam in Hebrew language in 7 lessons. Evening course for museum curating. Reuben Roshbari 054772692. (Not on the Sabbath)

—Delicatessen!!! Slow-cooked veal (sale). Kugel for Sabbaths! Hirsh Angel. 122/4 Muftar St

—Itzik Greenveld. Agent. Meat. Sausage. Oil. Charcoal. Lamark St. Shelter. East wing (sales on site).

Mr Johaness remembered everything. In his mind, he closed the box of cards, some from here, from when he tried to continue his beloved printing work in the new place, and some from there. That was the beginning of Mr Johaness' blindness.

* * *

Between the Johanesses' flat and our house were twenty-two steps. Going up and coming down. I counted them as we went up. I was weary of the nuisance of words. And the numbers seemed so desolate to me. I sought the desolation so I could bury myself in it.

Thus another day passed and I had made the bed before we went down, and now, when we returned, I fell into it as I passed by, and plunged into a deep sleep.

The next day is a short Friday and my husband goes out first thing in the morning to buy a Sabbath meal at the delicatessen which specializes in Sabbath dishes for Jerusalem residents, and I reached out to take the packet of pamphlets which my husband usually collects from them so I could place them on the shelf by the front door, in the place he had already set aside for them. I said to myself, I will read a few of them and see what they are about, and my husband honoured the day that the pamphlets came out, and every Friday while he was still praying in the synagogue, he would place the previous week's pamphlet in his coat pocket, although they were given freely to anyone who wanted them, and carried the word of the 'faithful' who occupied themselves in writing the short articles published in those pamphlets, and alongside them, new interpretations of the holy writers, as well as current events which the pamphlets were always full of, and the same 'faithful' occupied themselves also in the editing and distribution of the pamphlets.

And as I read, I saw how evil were the people of which the pamphlets spoke. The great evil of Hagar, Abraham's maidservant, so that he finally cast her away to the desert.[9] And her only son thirsted in the desert until the angel of God forgave him his sin. And Ishmael—*his hand will be against every man, and every man's hand against him*[10]—the Lord gave us an evil neighbour and we did not know. The Lord has made a laughing stock of us. And Ishmael laughed before Isaac. Laughed at Isaac. Both of them laughed, one with a good laugh, and the other with an evil laugh. And Jacob was a hero. Who gave him the strength to roll the boulder off the well? A single shepherd from among our forefathers did something that many Gentile shepherds

9 Genesis 21:8–21, King James Bible.
10 Genesis 16:12, King James Bible.

together could not do. And after that we were born. Korach[11] was evil, but even so he found himself follow-ers. They were called 'Korach's gang'. Korach and his gang argued against Moses. Those that injure a righteous man will end up with the righteous man attacking them with a cane of destruction. Korach dis-appeared. But the spies[12] did not disappear. The Amalekites[13] did not disappear. And Amalek is Haman. And the spies will conquer the Amalekites, whose evil is the worst of all, enormous, greater than any other evil in the world.

At the Makov Family

I had enough of human evil and sought for myself a corner without evil. I went down to the courtyard and sat down on a bench that the municipality had pro-vided under an oak tree. A boy of about fifteen passed by. Up to then I had seen him occasionally stumbling by on crutches, for he was missing one leg below the

11 A Levite leader who instigated a failed rebellion against Moses (Numbers 16). His punishment was to be swallowed up by the earth.

12 The twelve tribal leaders sent to scout out the land of Canaan in preparation for the Israelites' entrance into the land. Ten of the twelve brought back negative reports which the Israelites believed (Numbers 13).

13 Members of Amalek, an ancient tribe identified throughout the Bible as a recurrent enemy of the Israelites (see Deuteronomy 25:17).

knee, and now here he was walking without crutches, with just a small cane or sort of single crutch to help him hop along.

One crutch is not a pair of crutches, I said to myself, so that is good. Here is some progress. I smiled at the boy to encourage him in his walking but he was not looking at me. I remained alone. I remembered that we were invited that evening to the Makov family, a couple originally from England, long-time members of the Ohel Sarah[14] synagogue. Mrs Makov introduced herself to me when I accompanied my husband to the synagogue on the last Hoshana Rabbah[15] holiday, and I noticed a paucity of expression, as though she had already properly married off all her sons and daughters and now she just wanted to be left in peace, since anyway she did not really like all the sons- and daughters-in-law who had joined her family, and what can you expect from the sons and daughters that they would produce? While the husband, Mr Makov, of whom it was said that he is a silent partner in the English department store Harrods, spends most of his free time listening to operas on sophisticated electronic equipment, while not listening to any other kind of music or even admitting its existence. But Mr Makov's unusual fascination with the world of opera, like his wife's dull expression, did not deter anyone who was

14 'Sarah's Tent'.

15 The last day of the seven-day Feast of Tabernacles (in Hebrew, *Sukkot*).

invited to their home. Indeed, you would still not find anyone in that small community in Jerusalem who would reject such an invitation.

Thus we, too, arrive at the home of the Makov family, since we have been invited. At seven-thirty we knock on their door and discover that we are actually neighbours, that our houses are only a stone's throw apart. Not more. We enter to a joyful greeting which is repeated with each successive guest's arrival. First they indicate chairs with rounded legs, Sit here, they say, next to the window. And already a slim girl with a steady hand brings us something that looks like wrinkled dried fruit. I look at the guests. The more I look at them, the more I try to hear their words, the more their words grate on my ears and their images blur. Only the mistress of the house speaks clearly. Above everyone else, she holds forth on the marvels of her travel agent, Aviva. For twenty years I have arranged trips only through her, but now the prices are going up everywhere before the holidays, you have to make travel reservations early. But not an aisle seat, never. The son Itzik presents himself to the guests. He became engaged last month and now he will don a black hat and a short caftan. Everyone is invited to the table. To the dining room, they say. I am seated next to the owner of a stationery store. The largest in Jerusalem, so he informs me. And my husband—next to the Nechushtans. Yes, yes, Nechushtan lifts from Jerusalem. Does everyone count himself as an opera lover? *And two bears came out of the woods . . .*[16] The hostess eyes the seated guests narrowly. Here they will eat my food and drink from my glasses and won't leave us anything—and meanwhile, eggplant salad and vegetarian chopped liver are brought to the table—and I will give them the milk that has soured and they will take custody of it in their stomachs. Their stomachs are stuffed, she says to herself, and adds aloud: Cursed are the ignoramuses here! They are all Ishmaelites. How well did our blessed forefathers know to depict the future. And Isaac and Ishmael have come to us again! Everything is starting again! And the owner of the largest stationery store in Jerusalem, located on Ussishkin Street, repeats the hostess' words as his ear caught them: 'Does whatever he wants!' And the hostess hears the store owner's words, and repeats them, for now they are her words too: 'Does whatever he wants!' And the whole government follows him and the country is going to the dogs!! And I know who they were talking about, and I feel like tearing off a page from the little notebook I might find in my bag, or if it is not there—I will tear it from the little calendar, and I will write on it: *Save me for I am trapped in a snake's nest*, and I will add three exclamation points and throw the note out the window as if it were a child's parachute or paper aeroplane, and it will float along until it lands, just in case a saviour might show up. And I look up at the

16 II King 2:24, first half. The verse ends 'and mauled forty-two of them'.

people sitting there, and their voices are melding into one another, and their images are merging before my eyes, perhaps because of the distance, I say to myself, and then he says: To make himself a place in the society if . . . Like mushrooms sprouting up after rain, someone else answers. And when are we going to the Feldmans? Card games? No card games. I hear, There is a good show at the Cameri theatre. No, not to *Hamlet* or to *The Producers* . . . And foreign shows have been cancelled anyway. Not at the Feldmans, not on the Sabbath. Since their grandfather died, they observe the Sabbath. And have you already gone to the Clausels? And what are you talking about? You bathe once a year . . . Really, don't talk to me like that, I am not an Arab . . . You are not an Arab, really . . .

What are you twittering about? Arabs were here before you, I hear myself break in suddenly. The store owner from Ussishkin Street raises his head. Silence falls. I think: Perhaps in the meantime someone will find the note . . . Maybe someone will come and rescue me from here . . . And suddenly, a chemist from the Passiflora Fertilizer Company: The young lady is right. He looks towards me. What is your name, madam? I didn't catch your name when we were introduced. But what does that matter now? Loud voices arise, swallowing up my name as it is weakly handed over. There is no point to all this. A Bible teacher who was sitting among the guests at the table—I did not notice him until then—says: Archaeology has already proven that

Philistines are Philistines, and Palestinians is a bas-
tardized name for Philistines, and DNA testing proves
that they are not a sea people, and they did not arrive
here from Asia Minor but, rather, they are Philistines
who are Palestinians, he said. The Holy One Blessed Be
He has brought us a historical enemy, and thus I taught
my students, and the Bible teacher begins to chant a sort
of victory song, and the word 'enemy' in Hebrew is an
anagram for 'Job', and he added to the words of the song,
'and what is Job's fate?' I taught my students . . . —And
if they are Philistines, I cut off the teacher's words, why
don't you leave them alone and let them settle in
Philistine? And after that they discuss auto insurance
for a Peugeot, but from the moment I intervened in the
conversation, my husband looked right through me as
though I was not there and thus it continued throughout the rest of the evening, and even as we walked
home together. The whole way home.

Mr Shapira Young and Old

The path leading from our entrance curves around
strangely, first to the north, because the entrance to the
house faces north, and afterwards, making a sort of
about-face, it turns south, and finally towards the
southeast, and there it crosses an abandoned lot, at
whose edge stands the building in which Mr Shapira
lives. A rather bleak building, almost bitter, like its

owner, Mr Shapira, a house built at a time when locals did not worry about beauty or completing details with precision or attention, for what did these matter in comparison with really important things? And thus Mr Shapira spends his later years, his old age, not in poverty but in extreme modesty, and this despite the fact that at a distance of ten steps, not more, lives his daughter, Miriam Eybeschutz, our neighbour from the third floor, in some comfort, in a well-kept building, from which she leaves for her busy workdays in Romema and after that in French Hill and after that returns home, agitated by the news of the preceding day, which is always bad and infuriating, and then she turns to the rest of the tasks awaiting her that day, which include boiling and frying and light ironing and tidying up objects which have been scattered since yesterday and putting them back in place, and finally, late in the evening, she moves the rectangular dining table at which I sat when she invited us to Sabbath meals in her home, and pulls the couch towards her until it becomes a perfectly adequate bed, and makes it up with pillows and sheets and blankets until it becomes a double bed, and turns to the bathroom and readies herself for a short night's sleep which she also treats as an obligation the world demands from her, and dreams of the mayor who accompanies her, and perhaps she accompanies him, to visit her elderly father, and she holds a small crock of pea soup in her hands and steam is rising from it, and ladles out a generous portion for Mr Shapira, and meanwhile turns her head towards the mayor, who is already surrounded by an entourage of two assistants and a small secretary. And sometimes Mr Shapira appears, while still in the dream, as a young man with a tanned face, and he dances around the walls and holds a surprise for her in his hand, and his hand is held high over his head. How his daughter waited expectantly then for him to bend his head towards her and embrace her.

Many years ago, the young Shapira was hired to work at the Interior Ministry. At first he worked in the Jewish Agency because there was no state yet, and an office not yet called the Interior Ministry dealt with internal affairs, but afterwards everything worked out and the state was declared to exist, and that office formally became the Interior Ministry, and the young Shapira still worked there, at first only half-time and even as a courier who was required to deliver urgent and sometimes classified mail or to arrange something in more distant post offices, parcel post for example, or to wait in line for the teller at one of the banks (where there was a constant queue of impatient people), and because all these missions were important, and fulfilling them required responsibility and good judgement, and since the young Shapira did not own a bicycle and perhaps because of that did not know how to ride one, he began carrying out his missions with the help of car services (which at that time were called in Hebrew by the English word 'taxi'), anyway, the young Shapira taught himself to stop taxis quickly and efficiently, because that also requires skill, and even today senior department managers, particularly department managers at a bank, do not know how to stop a simple taxi, and when occasionally they are forced to do it—a common person squeezes in and takes his place on the seat before they can even think of what exactly to say to the driver, and which street in Petach Tikvah they want to get to.

One morning, young Shapira awoke feeling strange. His nightclothes clung to his body. I guess I must have sweated, he said. I guess I must have sweated a lot. Then he remembered that he had dreamt about something, something different and foreign and even distant. But this something, that is, the dream, came closer and closer to him as time passed, and some time about noon, everything became clear in his head, clear and organized, for even then young Shapira was an orderly person who did not tend to leave things unclear or let them slip away until they were entirely lost. In the dream, the young Shapira leant over an abandoned, half-ruined grave, as though he was seeking something and did not know what, and while he was still leaning there, now towards a mound of ruins which had suddenly sprouted over the abandoned grave, he heard a voice calling his name: Shapira!! Sha—pi—ra!! (To be precise, the voice pronounced his name badly, so that the word he heard was actually 'Shapila', but young Shapira chose to ignore this and kept the dream in his memory as though it were correct) and young Shapira said to himself: After all, I know my name, and thus he asked: What is your wish? And added: What do you want from me, O departed one? For his imagination could only grasp the image of a wandering soul, a bit depressed and in need of help, of whose kin he had heard and read about in various stories.—What is your wish, O lost soul? he asked again, and the voice answered: I am no lost soul, but the Judge Otniel Ben Knaz! A respected judge from the ancient days of the judges who ruled the people! Thus shall you address me! I command you to repair a grievous injury! They have destroyed my grave! My headstone has disappeared. Ruinous feet have trodden over my body. I command you to begin work immediately!! There was no room for doubt. Young Shapira was shaking and his nightclothes were sticking to his body. Everything became clear. It was impossible not to obey. From now on, he would need to change the scenery. No more rushed taxi rides on errands at the manager's beck and call, but works of organization and super-vision that would be centred in the office. And efficiency above all, young Shapira said to himself. Enough of the idle life! There are plans to be carried out and they await him within the inner workings of the mechanism itself. A year passed and Shapira became one of the junior staff members in the Interior Ministry. He was recommended by no other than the purchaser of our office supplies, Doctor Liddleman. He, as owner of a certain franchise, would show up at various government offices excessively burdened with packages and bags. He would unpack the packages little by little, and only at the customer's demand, and after he had convinced himself that it was indeed not for nothing, he would deign to unload his burden before the customer. For the load, when the cords tied around it were loosened, tended to get scattered about the room with nothing to stop it, first by falling, and then, with the help of the young secretaries who tended to adopt some of the contents for themselves, particularly pens, colourful staplers or office ashtrays that would routinely disappear within a short time. Doctor Liddleman also sold typewriter paper, and this particularly weighed him down, and when he dropped his load on a chair he would extract from the pocket of his grey pants a large, wrinkled handkerchief and wipe the sweat from his face and neck. One of the secretaries offered him a drink of water. A cup was brought, but the water was not cold and Doctor Liddleman scarcely drank. After the first sip, he did not take any more, and perhaps the water tasted to him of mould, for tap water in the country was not pure and Doctor Liddleman was sensitive to such things. He was a good man, and in remembering the exhausted figure of young Shapira now running around the streets of Jerusalem to fulfil his errands, while here young people sit, at their side infantile secretaries wasting the government's money on 'coffee breaks' and 'cigarette breaks' and lately he heard that they agreed here to 'breaks to repair fingernails damaged during typing', and these were deceitfully used for nail trimming and various manicures, and thus a heavy smell of nail polish and acetone constantly hung in the air of all government offices at that time, his natural sense of justice was offended, and Doctor Liddleman dwelled on that, and also on the perpetual absence of the youth Shapira 'Because he has to run around the smoky streets,' as he told the manager, as he opened his receipt book, 'and he is a particularly successful boy,' he added, and then: 'one of the most successful I have ever met,' and the manager was impressed. Matters percolated slowly, and Doctor Liddleman repeated his words, more than once or twice, and each time to another manager, until the opportunity arose and young Shapira was accepted as a member of the internal staff of the Interior Ministry, and then as a member of the junior management team established there, for warm words of recommendation have real power, and particularly when the recommender bears the title of Doctor. But Doctor Liddleman also remembered that more than once, on particularly hot summer days (that is, most summer days), or on stormy winter days, he would hear young Shapira's voice floating out from the open window of a passing taxi, inviting him to get inside. 'And put the things inside too,' would strengthen his heart, 'We will bring you to wherever you need to go. Where do you need to go today, Doctor Liddleman? Which office are you going to now?' And after that he would address the driver: 'Right, Itzik? We have good work today!' For young Shapira had a special arrangement with the taxi drivers, they would give him receipts for his payments (in those days, a new and almost unheard-of custom), while he, Shapira, would hand the receipts to the man at the information desk located at the entrance to the office building, and every two weeks he would receive cash back for them, and once or twice what he received was more than what was written on the receipts.

Shapira's generous nature did not flag when he became an adult and an old man. His work at the Interior Ministry progressed well, until it became an inseparable part of him. More and more people were pronouncing the words 'Interior Ministry', and immediately adding the words 'Mr Shapira', and vice versa. When they said 'Mr Shapira', they would immediately add the words 'Interior Ministry' and even Mr Shapira himself, when he would say his name to someone, would immediately add 'Interior Ministry'. Thus, for example, when he called to order a refill of cooking gas for his flat, or in common parlance, 'to order a bottle of gas', he was wont to say, 'Hello, this is Shapira speaking from the Interior Ministry. I would like to order a new bottle of gas.' Then the clerk would say: New as a replacement or new in addition? Or she would ask: Completely full or full only in the lower section, Mr Shapira? And Mr Shapira was pleased. And all that time, his work bore fruit and the Interior Ministry expanded its spheres of activity and sometimes stepped outside the familiar and publicly acceptable boundaries, and got involved with other matters, like work on the Sabbath, emigration, conversion and marriage.

And only after some time (months, and perhaps a year or two)—for Shapira had learnt to be cautious, unlike in his taxi days—he addressed himself to restoring the grave of Judge Otniel Ben Knaz as he had been commanded in his dream (for everything had started there), and only after that went on to restore additional graves, starting with the forefathers mentioned in the Scriptures and ending with recently discovered graves of righteous men. In this way, he was wont to say, the generations will come close to each other, living and dead, and the unity of the people will grow, and also holy ground in our country will increase in area and not be handed over to strangers, so everything is for the good. In his secret thoughts he hoped to discover the graves of Deborah the Prophetess and Barak son of Avinoam, and hoped to find them next to each other even though he knew that was impossible, and he felt sorry for the prophet Micah, perhaps because he did not get very many chapters in the Bible, 'and he deserves more,' he thought. Then he thought about the great prophets: Isaiah, Jeremiah and about the tragic kings Yehoyakim, Yehoyakin, and tears filled his eyes. He had to work quickly if he was to restore everyone's graves, and yet felt that he would not have time. It's beyond my strength, he felt, but I will try, I will do everything . . . everything I can . . . he promised to someone, not even to himself, to someone more elevated and important.

When almost forty years of work had passed, General Director Shapira left behind him 468 graves solidly identified, properly fixed up and cared for, with access paths and low shrubs that put forth white blossoms on clear winter days, and 250 more graves about which there was some doubt. As for the ones that were certain—their names were recorded on Israeli Carta maps and a certain government office accorded them a permanent budget, with the Interior Ministry's encouragement but not on its behalf. Thus the adult Shapira had become clever and thus had he changed with time. But the graves which were in doubt did not receive anything. They would have to wait until they were thoroughly discussed at the various ministries. And meanwhile, only neighbours and residents of nearby villages would bring them scattered flowers, lying for some time among them with outstretched arms as though hugging someone, and sobbing.

Those days were beautiful to the elderly Shapira, and worthy of praise. But they too passed, for such is the way of the world that all passes and is gone, and for the elderly Shapira came a time in which he was no longer called Old Shapira but, rather, Very Old Shapira or Shapira the Ancient, and he did not spend his days in spacious offices with windows made for tending houseplants and fresh flowers that were changed every two days, but, rather, in an extremely modest flat in a gloomy building. He lives on the second floor, and they refer to him as 'the pensioner'. That's the pensioner from the floor above, and not: that's our General Director, and so on . . . And his wife is no longer at his side because she has left this world, and of all his children scattered in various countries remains only one daughter, named Miriam Eybeschutz, taking her name from her husband who is a descendant of the learned Eybeschutz who left behind great turmoil among Hasidim and Misnagdim,[17] and she lives near her father and watches over his doings from some distance, and her thoughts turn to him more than once.

Miriam Eybeschutz is an energetic woman. Her son, a yeshiva student from Gush Katif, though still a youth, works tirelessly to bring to fruition visions of the great homeland, visions to which his grandfather also clung. Miriam is proud of him, and it is important not to play down this pride. Because of 'the righteousness of the way', as she said. In her house she entertains famous guests: a popular watchdog over the Hebrew language who ran regular radio and television spots in which he was wont to root out errors by properly denouncing familiar rhymes and songs which actually spread these errors more widely, because of popular inattention and ignorance; an expert in packing paper whose samples were accepted for sale in the European Soho; a director of Jewish films who has acquired world renown; of all these she maintains awareness, while she herself has started an ambitious project, on both municipal and national levels, to prepare the jubilee celebration for the walled city of Jerusalem, so

17 Members of two movements among Eastern European Jewry, from the eighteenth century on.

that she is also one of the famous, and her guests do not feel that they are lowering themselves in any way when they are invited to her home. At these small gatherings she finds herself a public which shows interest and even curiosity about the festivities with which Jerusalem will soon be inundated, and she takes it on herself not to allow these festivities to end too quickly (it would take nearly a year to celebrate Jerusalem properly) and she promises that 'one celebration will follow another', and all this will be accompanied by street performances for which dozens of clowns have already been recruited. One of her guests proposes that by rights she should be granted the Israel Prize, and then they ask, What is the prize for—contribution to society or to the Jewish people? For Jerusalem is tied to all the Jews in the Diaspora, not only the Jews living in Israel. It is very pleasant to be a guest of the Eybeschutz family and it is pleasant to Miriam and her husband to receive such pleasant guests. They sip tea, admire one another's stories, laugh briefly when appropriate and sigh sadly at less opportune events. In short, they fulfil their role as good guests.

It is the day after one of the pleasant gatherings at her home, and Miriam is going out, as she does three or four times a week 'to supplement the shopping'. In the small shops on Palmach Street shopkeepers compliment her: Madam Miriam, how well you look! When will you finally decide to age a little? And others say, We saw you on television this week. When was it, maybe Monday or Tuesday? And Miriam is pleased. And she is more pleased than usual after an evening 'event' which went over so well, and people reacted so positively to it later on the telephone as well. Those days were good to Miriam, but bad to elderly Mr Shapira, her father. For starters, he did not like old age and it did not suit him at all. Pleasant gatherings of guests did not visit *his* flat, and no one said to him when he went to buy white bread, Mr Shapira, we saw you yesterday on television, good job! He himself said more than once: I don't need all this, and also: I don't miss having lots of people around me, and instead he talked a lot about his grandson who was studying in Gush Katif and thereby serving the state, and people he met on the way would listen to him politely, mainly when he mentioned his grandson's grades for the second trimester, which he had memorized and could recite in the correct order, from Mishnah[18] and Halacha[19] to advanced mathematics. At this stage the listener would usually say: Very interesting, Mr Shapira, you have a very successful grandson. And after he had stopped the grandfather's flood of words with this comment, the listener would find an excuse to escape the place and never return. And thus the elderly Shapira was left most of the time alone, without the audience he was used to, and without those words that were once constantly with him, and that generally

18 First part of the Jewish oral tradition.

19 Jewish law.

expressed agreement, obedience and praise for his wisdom and efficiency. Those were not easy days for the elderly Shapira, but in some way he made peace with them, for he had no choice, and not a few laid this to his credit, that 'Old Shapira doesn't give in to old age' and 'He still has amazing powers.'

His daily schedule was more or less this: In the morning, he would get up at sunrise, pray, dress, drink some boiled water with honey, and sit himself down before his beloved books, holy books all, and read them inside and out, sometimes seeking references and citations from the Midrash[20]—he particularly liked Midrash Rabbah—and then he would take a break for breakfast which would include slices of tomato, a slice of matza[21] spread with Tnuva white cheese, and a cup of weak coffee. He had learnt to take care of himself a bit and prepare simple meals. In the afternoon he would open two plastic boxes with which his daughter had carefully stocked his large refrigerator, full of cooked foods, and would heat himself up a meat pastry and some vegetables. Evenings and holidays were somewhat problematic. He would go out walking alone on sunny days, and on Friday he would go to synagogue, but when darkness fell and bedtime arrived,

20 Ancient commentaries on parts of the Bible. Midrash Rabbah is a specific collection of these commentaries.

21 A flat, dry bread, made solely of flour and water, primarily eaten by Jews during the Passover holiday, when leaven is forbidden.

he did not have the strength to bathe and prepare himself for sleep. This was a problem, and two yeshiva boys were summoned to his house to help him. They were studying in the yeshiva opposite his house, and they viewed it as a mitzvah.[22] Therefore a duty roster was set up. Different yeshiva students would arrive each evening, and Mr Shapira gave up trying to identify their faces, and would recognize them only by the clothes they wore, which always had the same familiar look, easily identified. As for holidays, following the same duty roster, yeshiva students would come on Fridays and holiday eves (then they would also shake out the bedclothes, change the sheets and dust the furniture). One of them would take care of restocking the matza in the kitchen, for as the days passed Shapira denied himself various foods which he termed 'poison', until he was eating nothing but matza with cheese and jam and had become weary of everything else.

At about six o'clock in the evening the yeshiva students would arrive. Usually they would move rapidly, a habit they had acquired during their long period of studies. One of them would go to the kitchen and put up an egg to boil in a small pot, just in case today Mr Shapira might agree to eat a soft-boiled egg as well. One would light the electric boiler for exactly twenty minutes. The two of them would devote half an hour

22 From the Hebrew root 'to command'. A mitzvah can be a specific commandment from the Torah, but it can also refer to any good deed.

to the old man's bath, and after that would dress him and fold his clothes. They would place them on the chair next to his bed. He would brush his teeth and wash his face on his own. They would soap his body with moisturizing soap and then rinse him with warm water and take him to his bed. He had not yet gone to the bathroom. After that he would say the bedtime prayer, still sitting up, and then allow himself to slide slowly among the pillows and blankets.

The yeshiva students leave. Quietly they close the door on their way out and lock it from outside. It is dark in the flat, but Shapira has a spare set of keys. In the dark, he gropes for the switch to turn on the small lamp. He sits down again and listens until the yeshiva students' voices in the stairwell and the street die away. They are still discussing an egg which was laid on the Sabbath, Shapira mutters something scornful, and then from the bed he lowers one thin leg to the floor and waits. My legs no longer carry me, he derides himself, and almost jumps up by pushing off with the second leg, and forward into the thick, long underwear—cool Jerusalem nights. Shapira dresses rapidly. The weariness has disappeared. At ten minutes after twelve, the taxi will arrive. I ordered it, I ordered it, as though playing defence attorney for himself. His small abdomen is bloated. Too much matza, too many disgusting foods. This is a 'dry and thirsty land',[23] but there

23 Hosea 13:5: 'I took care of you in the wilderness, in that dry and thirsty land.'

is a compensation. There is a small compensation,
Shapira smiles as though he has managed to outsmart
a few people around him. The briefcase and the paper-
work are packed. Before it got dark I packed myself a
small package, he hums to himself and adds a sharpened pencil to the package. The title at the top of the
first page reads: 'Since when have Lag b'Omer[24] bonfires
become a commandment from the Torah?' He hurries.
He locks everything. A medium-sized cat in quiet
patent-leather shoes. The taxi is already here, blinking
among the bushes.—Turn off your engine, he commands it silently. The driver had better not honk.
Having already acquired a cat's tread, he is off. In
Sanhedria,[25] in a basement, a group of young people
would be waiting for him, enthusiastic men and
women. All of them in the advanced stages of becoming
religious, and they are known as the 'Rabbi Shimon
Bar Yochai Group'.[26] Rabbi Shapira—thus they address
him—teaches them the meaning of the laws from the
holy books, and he has already prepared ten lectures on
this topic alone. Afterwards they bring him home in a

24 A holiday named for the thirty-third day of the Omer, a forty-
nine-day period between Passover and the Feast of Weeks. This
holiday is traditionally celebrated by lighting bonfires.

25 An ultra-orthodox neighbourhood of Jerusalem.

26 A famous mystical rabbi from the second century CE, active
after the destruction of the Second Temple in Jerusalem. The
anniversary of his death falls on Lag b'Omer, which is one of the
reasons for the celebrations on that day.

taxi, accompanying him to his house. Cool Jerusalem air.—Dear Rivka, he whispers to his dead wife, I was wonderful . . . I am coming . . . I am going to bed . . . Sleep, you sleep there . . . And then he corrects himself: May your sleep be sweet, he says. Now he feels himself close to the world of the dead. He has become so alive.

Old Shapira goes out to lectures almost every other evening. One evening he gives a lecture, and on the next he rests and lets his body recover some strength. The newly religious like night-time lectures. They carry with them an atmosphere of secrecy, perhaps of mystery, and mainly, of a cult, a persecuted and holy cult. But all this is more or less understood. And Shapira? Is he not too old for games?—First of all, these are not games. Second, he is not old, not old at all.

The Russian Woman

And now again: Here I am. And here is my husband. My husband knew old Shapira long before he heard my name, for he had been a neighbour and father to good neighbours in the building where he lived. Thus Mr Shapira had always been in the background of our acquaintance. At first in the background, and then moved to the foreground, slowly forward into the centre. At first he served as a sort of teacher to my husband on minor halachic questions which my husband would pose to him, such as: How do you make an eruv[27] in the home when there is no woman at home, a helpmate to make the eruv? And: Is it permitted to sew on a loose button on Saturday night after the Sabbath, when righteous women would not sew on Saturday nights? Old Shapira spoke to my husband warmly and patiently, and my husband, with his questions which preserved a measure of respect for the rabbi, became dear to his heart.

Later, he shared with him matters of the heart. My husband met a Russian woman. A doctor from Moscow. It seems that she has a child, he is not sure. Yes, yes, fifteen years old. Perhaps thirteen. My husband writes in his appointment book: Find out about the son. Old Shapira says: Is there a child or not? That's actually an important issue. My husband thinks: It's good that there is someone to consult with. An older man, wiser, a friend. Then they go fishing together. Not to fish, to sit on the porch, to chat. As though they are fishing. They look at the world. Shapira tells the story of his life and things that happened to him. My husband is impressed: Each time I become more of a believer in the Creator of the world and our right to this land. It's wonderful. The meaning of these things is hidden from us until the End of Days, my husband

27 From the root 'commixture'. A construct in Jewish law which enables one to prepare for the Sabbath on a holiday, in a case where the holiday immediately precedes the Sabbath.

says, and Shapira looks at him with agreement. They become friends.

And the Russian woman? The Russian woman is caring for an elderly man not far from here, just a stone's throw past the corner of Alkalai Street. She does everything. Cooking, light housework, changing diapers. And the son? Does she have a son? Does she have a mother? Enough, enough. After a few weeks: We have to help the Russian woman. Working for the elderly man is bad for her. Yes, she has a place to sleep, but in the meantime she will sleep here.—Here? That means in my flat, my husband says and grins. First thing is to find her a normal job, her old man already does nothing but frown. Shapira proposes: A hospital. After all, you are a doctor.

And my husband begins his search. It is hard for him. He has not been in the country very long either and he does not speak Hebrew well. He asks at Hadassah Hospital. Yes. They need a doctor. Perhaps she is a paediatrician? What is her speciality? And Sonia (Sonia? Yes) is hired at Hadassah. In the end my husband did help. At least, it is better than taking care of the old man. And Sonia moves into my husband's flat. He introduces her to his friend from Hadera and his wife. His friend has ordination to work in the Rabbinate. Do you want me to marry you two? the friend from Hadera asks, It's not good to live together without a marriage ceremony. These days people do things like that, the friend from Hadera continues, just for the Torah. Without the Interior Ministry, without the state, what do you care . . . My husband hesitates, Sonia stands next to him and listens. We'll discuss it by telephone, my husband finally says, I need to think about it all. Sonia is a size thirty-six. So little. You could buy her clothes in a children's clothing store. But slender she is not. Not slender enough.

Sonia has been hired to work at Hadassah, and it appears that she is not a doctor. The documentation did not arrive from Moscow. It was sent from the old university but did not arrive. OK, then I will be a nurse, she says. But here, too, there is a matter of documentation and she has no documentation. And Dr Caspi from Neurosurgery agrees: she will be an assistant, an uncertified nurse, and take a course in the Nursing School. The course has already started. Evening classes three times a week. My husband records the hours and days in his notebook, and the work days—in green ink. Thus he oversees everything. And then they travel together to a boarding house in Sde Yoav. All this he tells his new friend, Shapira.—It's not good, that it should happen to you . . . Not good . . . —But you too . . . My husband begins and then breaks off. No, I won't hurt a friend. And then he invites Sonia to join him— Let's go see how old Shapira is doing, how does he spend his Sabbaths alone, he says . . . and there, two yeshiva students like two scoundrels from Hell. In black clothes. They are so fast. One is brandishing a fly swatter at a mosquito drowsing on the wall and the second manages to hit it with the palm of his hand. A bit of blood is smeared on the wall, a drop of human blood that passed to a mosquito, smeared on the wall of Mr Shapira's home. And after all it is a drop of human blood, and the second yeshiva student takes out a wrinkled handkerchief from his pocket, sprays it with his saliva, and wipes the wall. Wipes and smears further the drop of blood which had spread out and not faded away. And now what? Now he spits on the wall. For nothing. For nothing. But the friend Shapira looks at Sonia: She's pretty. Cute. But what? I will tell you later, what will happen to you. It doesn't suit you to be with someone who lied . . . —But you . . . my husband says again and breaks off. That's right, he knows . . . the end justifies the means . . . but not every end, only a good end like the integrity of the land of Israel and commitment to God's word. But how is Sonia's purpose bad? Sonichka who wanted only good for herself and her son. For now it turns out that she has a son and he is fourteen years old. But Shapira shakes his head, nods and says: Let it be . . .

And thus more days pass. The Russian woman is no longer around. They have split up. Once they went to the Israel Museum. My husband invited her. Sonia stood there and held forth about Chagall. They brought some of Chagall's paintings from France. Sonia stood there and held forth: The colours are beautiful. The subjects are not beautiful.—What do you mean, the subjects are not beautiful? My husband's face darkened.

Since when does one judge works of art by their subjects? Sonia was undeterred: Perhaps here one does not judge, but I studied art in Moscow, and there they judge and how. This is already too much, my husband thought and did not say a word. This I am not going to tell Shapira . . . He does not understand such subtleties . . . And in his heart he decided to end the relationship. After that came the throat pain. My husband tended to get sick with sore throats. And Sonia brought him food. It turns out that she had gone back to living in the old man's house, but had not taken her belongings from my husband's house.—It turns out that she now has two toothbrushes, my husband said, grinning . . . Who knows . . . And the meals packed so nicely—a meal for each day—he got angry at them and put them in the freezer. Some time after we got married, he suggested heating up one of them each day, and we would have food for a whole week.

So they returned from the museum. It was a winter day, and my husband realized that he had lost one of his light-coloured leather gloves. And one glove is not enough, it is as though he lost both gloves. In his diary he wrote: I lost one glove. At the end of the day he wrote it, at the bottom edge of the page. And then he understood that the loss of the glove was somehow connected to Sonia's speech before Chagall's painting. An ancient anger arose in him, and he would not be consoled for the loss of the glove, and then we met each other. I had some issue then with the Bank of

Israel. The bank in the neighbourhood where I lived had given me ample credit and did not demand that I pay off the debt. Except for polite notices that arrived from time to time mentioning the debt, the matter did not arise at all, as though there was no real need to pay off the debt. And then suddenly there was a need. And what's more, immediately. Perhaps a new manager came in, or a new law had been passed in the country, and I had to travel to Jerusalem to present my case before an authorized clerk from the Central Bank.

I wandered the corridors of the bank for some time, searching for the clerk in charge of my case. Although to be precise, they were not exactly corridors but more like alleys, for the bank had been built according to the new model of the Museum of Modern Art which had recently opened in New York, and its corridors were bounded by a sparkling metal rail facing the centre, and they were placed one on top of the other like layers of an airy cake, and the doors to the rooms, some open and some closed, as though hinting at something. And here on the third floor, a narrow desk against the wall with a chair next to it, and on the chair, with her face to the wall and her back to the corridor, sat a bank clerk typing letters in English, because those are also needed at the Central Bank, I thought. And she typed faster than I could have imagined, and she did not turn her head, neither left nor right, lest she become distracted by the requests and questions of passers-by. I was about to ask her also about the location of the clerk in charge of my case, in case she might know the answer, but I stopped myself when, glancing quickly from the side, I saw a fine beard, long and narrow, cascading from the typist's chin, interwoven with a few grey hairs. I thought the beard nice enough but it did not seem to me that it suited the face of the English typist, for we were not used to such things where I came from. And it occurred to me that perhaps she had rebelled, and would not shave off her beard as the bank directors had instructed, and thus was being punished and her office was taken from her and from now on she would be excluded from the public view.

In this corridor I met my husband for the first time. He was also trying to find his way on the third floor, he also needed the signature of the same authorized clerk—the signature I was seeking, but for a different reason, for he needed to renew his license to import foreign currency into his account from his previous homeland without paying taxes on it, and thus we met. He did not notice the bearded typist, and since I passed him and did not have a beard on my chin, he asked me how to find that authorized clerk and from then on did not let me go, even if the expression 'did not let me go' is a bit exaggerated: my husband watched me as I passed by and from then on he did not leave my sight.

In those days his relations with women left him no satisfaction. The caretaker of the synagogue, the one who spoke ancient Russian, was seeking a suitable wife for him. And he even looked in the Russian newspapers which were published in Israel at that time. It was this caretaker who had brought to his attention the figure of the little Sonia, with whom my husband was much taken at first, and he told a few of his acquaintances from the small Swedish community, that now he has a new friend, a doctor from Russia, and later she no longer pleased him at all for she pretended to be an art expert and passed judgement when she should have been silent, only watching and listening, and 'that was a lot', and 'that was way too much'. Sonia ceased to find favour in my husband's eyes, but he did not cease to wonder about her activities, how she was managing there with the new work and studies, if she had gone back to living with the old man, and what she wore every day if most of her clothes remained in the two drawers that he had set aside for her in his large clothes closet and she was not bothering to come pick them up and take them to her place. He aired his concerns with his friend with the rabbinical certification from Hadera, who shared his pain: Give her a nice farewell gift (the friend meant a monetary gift) and rest assured. And the rest of my husband's troubles he resolved as pangs of conscience which would disappear with the gift and therefore were not important. But my husband understood very well what his friend saw as conscience and what the friend from Hadera meant, and even so said to himself: I will try one more time. Even by telephone. At least ask how she is doing. My husband was determined: Yes . . . Yes . . . No . . . The sore throat had passed (for he had become sick and gotten well again). Yes, thank you . . . Yes, for the food you brought. You didn't have to do it, you know my opinions on the subject, even if you were only fulfilling a woman's purpose in doing so. No . . . not her real purpose (which is always tied to birth, nursing, caring for children, etc. This sentence he did not speak aloud so as not to insult Sonia, and only spoke it soundlessly to himself) but, rather, what she sees as her purpose, since she is a being influenced and shaped by social prejudices, that is . . . to take care of a man, and I don't like this pretence . . .

—What pretence?

—I mean yours to yourself: I am a woman and I *must* make sure that he has enough food.

—No, I don't think that, Sonia answered because she did not understand my husband's thinking.

—So, how are you doing in general?

—And Sonia says: Fine, everything is fine. I'm having fun . . .

—Goodbye, my husband says.

Now he feels a little better. 'Having fun,' he repeats to himself. I do not need a woman who *has fun*. I try to find out how she's doing, and she's *having fun*. He repeats the phrase aloud a few times as though baring his woes before a nameless listener. He did not try again to find out how little Sonia was doing. And when the caretaker of the faraway synagogue asked him: So, what's with the woman you were set up with? he answered briefly: She's having fun. He did not elaborate. And her coffee mug, from which she used to drink when she visited my husband, he hung on a hook on the kitchen wall, so that he would not drink from it by mistake.

People can be divided into two categories. There are two main types of people. That I will find out today. One—large and constantly getting larger; and two—not large and does not shrink but, rather, remains the same size as time passes. A man leaves his house in the morning. His forehead is furrowed. He hides a folded white handkerchief in his pocket. He clings to the manners of another time. On the way he follows a line of larks walking one after another. The line unravels and the man says to himself: Soon it will be winter, or: Soon it will be summer. He turns up his collar. Suddenly he is cold, he sees a youth of about fifteen, with a broken leg in a cast. The youth stumbles around a partially shaded bench. The man sits down on the shady part of the bench. He looks out at the horizon, hidden by the city buildings, and wonders whether he met that day's obligations. He does not remember how he got here, for he was going somewhere else . . . Later he goes up and down stairs. Sometimes steps are missing and he has to jump . . . Young women of tender years surround him. They leap easily over the missing steps, but he himself has many problems. He does not want stairs.

After the stairs there is a lot of water. He crosses water mottled with whitewash and fruit peels floating in it. The water is moving, even flowing rapidly. Hidden streams, underground. The man dips his foot in and his shoes slip off his feet, and he is no longer sure who is dead and who is alive when he thinks about the dead. The long-time secretary of the Academy who once explained to him how to get to these stairs, and he asked her how to get to these stairs, did she not die two years ago? Did he not see her once at the house of mourning for a common friend? Her and her daughter? He is no longer sure. He saw her daughter. And her—he is not sure. He says to himself: She was always strange. Acted strangely towards me. Nice and not nice, as though she boiled seawater in a pot made of salt, something I would not have done if I were her, and will never do, he thinks to himself and tries to pull himself together. I will get up and get myself together, he says to himself. I'm already getting back to myself. I shall not die, but live,[28] he repeats as he once learnt by heart, and goes into a store to buy bandages. He already knows what to do. He should have been at the pharmacy in the first place. To buy bandages for his fingers. And here there is a pharmacy right across the street, and he stops for a moment: Perhaps bandages are included in the list of banned products now? It seems to him that at the beginning of the month, bandages were added to the list of banned products. How to find out? Who can he

28 Psalms 118:17: 'I shall not die, but live.'

ask? There is no one here, and he has made a mistake
with the pharmacy. It is not a pharmacy but a large
Superpharm, writhing like a lizard, which has sprouted
up here. All the salespeople and service people are in
blue coats. Everyone looks the same to him, this one
just like that one, and not even the tiniest detail distin-
guishes one from the others. And if he were to let the
bandages go, here all his fingers are burnt and covered
with raised yellow blisters. And if he were to stay, and
buy a package of bandages, all the packages are large
and heavy to carry for they are meant for families and
he is a single man. If he were to buy a big package,
because he could not find a smaller one, he would go
up to the cash register, and the salesgirl would ask who
he is and what is your name, sir, and what is his house
number and flat number, and she would ask pleasantly
and he would answer pleasantly for where we come
from, we would never answer a salesgirl's questions in
anything but a pleasant manner. And she would record
all his answers in a notebook. And when the man
returned home with the package of bandages in his
hand—it would seem to him that the package was
growing in his hands as he walked, the number of bandages in the package increasing as he walked—and he
would open his flat door with the key meant for that
purpose, and there would be three people waiting for
him at the large dining table still cluttered with yesterday's dishes, two men and a woman, and they would be
dressed in civilian clothes and the package of bandages
would be in his hand. And thus his guilt would be

proven and he would not be able to hide or deny anything. You, sir, buy banned products when you shop?
the woman says, one of the three.—I did not know, the
man replies hesitantly, or, more accurately, stutters, for
something has become known, and he had thought
about this once, that he might someday bring home a
banned product and a ban had already appeared and he
did not know about it, and he would add despairingly:
I need bandages . . . and extend towards the woman his
infected, blistered fingers. The woman would look to
the left. 'I did not know' is not an extenuating circum-
stance, she would say. You should have known.—But
how? the man would ask, knowing at the same time that
even if he had asked the service people in the blue coats,
his name and other identifying information would have
been passed on to the salesgirl, and everything would
have happened exactly as it was happening now. And
thus I did not ask, and anyway everything is lost, he
would say to himself, and ask the three citizens, Can I
take it with me? meaning the package, as they would
accompany him downstairs to the car whose driver had
drowsed off in the meantime, for the three had waited
so long in his house for him to come back from his
shopping trip. A neighbour in a yellow coat would wit-
ness the whole scene, and she would turn her face to
the side as she passed by him towards the stairs, so as
not to see.

* * *

My husband promised blind Mr Johaness from the first floor that he would accompany him to morning prayers every day until his wife returned from her vacation. Mr Johaness' wife had gone to France to rest at her daughter's, for she was worn out from her heavy domestic responsibilities; since Mr Johaness had gone blind, the task of caring for a blind husband had fallen on her. Mr Johaness spoke French, but also Yiddish and a little Hebrew. My husband smiled pleasantly when he spoke to him, even though Mr Johaness could not see that he was smiling. But the voice of a smiling person is different from a cold-hearted person whose mouth cuts his words like a knife. Mr Johaness made his request and my husband consented but his face was frozen as he replied, though his mouth continued to smile, for my husband knew that Mr Johaness arose before dawn and joined those who prayed at dawn, the first shift for the morning prayers. My husband did not refuse Mr Johaness, but his face remained frozen. Once my husband tried to train himself to join the early risers, and he signed up for the dawn prayers in order to accustom himself to get by on less sleep. My husband tried to join the dawn prayers but held out for only a few weeks before he asked the synagogue caretaker to remove him from the list. And now, he reflected, he would need to show up for two more weeks, and that was assuming that Mr Johaness' wife returned safely from her vacation, and all this because it is impossible to say no to a blind man. My husband thought of Mr Johaness as a tough man. And the other people who pray the morning prayers at dawn were also tough, and he meant particularly Hananiah, an eighty-five-year-old man who came to us from Petach Tikva after he had lived alone for several decades in a little guard's booth. He tormented himself strangely at morning prayers, because every time he would open the book to pray, he would doze off after reading only two or three lines of text. And he would try to read standing up and would fall asleep standing up. In the end he started coming to our synagogue equipped with a cooler full of blocks of ice and he would take off his shoes and socks before the prayers began, wedge his feet into the cooler, and thus stay on his feet for the entire prayer without dozing off. My husband did not like Hananiah's method, perhaps because he himself might have used it if he had had this Hananiah's problem. Now he would have to see the soles of Hananiah's feet, and scrutinize the other ones who came to pray at dawn, for at least two weeks, my husband thought, but he did not say a word of all this to Mr Johaness.

A few days after these events, a young man came to our house. He belonged to the group of men who prayed together.—A twenty-five-year-old fellow and as solitary as a rock, my husband said, but not to his face. When he introduced him to me he said: His name is Mordechai, he is alone in Israel. And he turned to the young man: Have a seat, make yourself at home. And then: What will you have to drink? Would you like something alcoholic? Perhaps some schnapps? My husband was a wine connoisseur who knew all about types of wine and how to store them.

—No, I don't drink wine, says the young man.

—Not even at the Sabbath table for the blessing?

—For the Sabbath blessing, grape juice.

Now the young man looks at my husband trustingly, for my husband is already a familiar face. My husband turns to me: Can you offer him something? As if the kitchen is my kingdom and the wines—his country.—Coffee? Tea? I ask.—No, could I please just have some water, in a glass cup if possible? the young man says, for he observes the Jewish dietary laws very strictly, and I bring him water in a glass cup. My husband and the guest are already deep in conversation; 'Pesikta d'Rav Kahana',[29] I hear the gist of their words, and the young man waxes enthusiastic: All the Gentile peoples in the land must be destroyed . . . There are already signs of complete redemption . . . Not just anyone can announce the coming of the Messiah, but to announce the coming of the one who is going to announce, that is something that an ordinary person can do . . .

The young man has come here from France.—I travelled to the cold parts of the country, he recounts, to roll in the snow, and then I returned to the city and brought with me lumps of snow in my beard. The

29 'Verses of Rabbi Kahana', an ancient collection of *midrashim* (commentaries on the Bible).

young man has a luxuriant black beard. The yarmulke on his head covers tangled hair. His eyes are wild but somehow veiled. Masked by something I cannot identify.—And all this you learnt there? I join the conversation, one way or another. The young man does not react. Perhaps he does not speak with women. But he answers my husband's questions willingly.—So how did you roll in the snow? my husband asks.

—I rolled. The young man does not elaborate.

—In your clothes?

—Not in my clothes.

—Not in any clothes?

My husband gets up to pour himself some schnapps.—It's not made by Gentiles, he turns to the young man jokingly, maybe you'll have some after all?

—No, not in clothes at all. Before dawn. I rolled in the snow completely alone.

—Why, I ask.

—Listen, my husband says, I understand this, even if I seem to be making a joke of it. My grandfather used to go out before sunrise and dig a pit in the snow. Within the pit, the snow turned to water, and he would bathe in that water. Every Friday and Monday.

—Yes, said the young man. That's a nice custom.

—And my husband: But we don't really have snow here, though I wish we did. But it's always possible to get up early . . . to get up early to serve the Creator . . .

My husband is satisfied that at least yesterday, today, and tomorrow he is joining the ranks of the God-fearing by accompanying blind Mr Johaness to the synagogue and thus he too is rising early to serve the Creator and meriting to join the dawn prayers, and he forgets that he has ever been angry about it.

And again my husband: Can I offer you some fruit perhaps? We have seasonal fruit, it is healthy to eat fruit. Eat, eat, and my husband signals to me to bring a plate of fruit from the kitchen, and he adds to the young man: I am a doctor, you know . . .

—All right, the young man gives in, I could have a piece of fruit . . . and bites into a peach after saying the blessing over fruits, and adding the blessing over baked goods for good measure. He says the blessing with closed eyes. And some people add twigs, the young man goes on, as though just now remembering, in the same tone in which he just pronounced the blessing over baked goods, and they add twigs to stir sleepy limbs that have not yet awoken, so that they will not be slack in serving the Creator.

—That's not the Judaism I know, I say quietly, but the young man overhears.

—Perhaps Madam does not know, it is not her job *to know*, the young man addresses his words to the empty room, but only to fulfil important Jewish commandments, though all the commandments are equally important because all come from a single source, and this contains great secrets and mysteries which Madam also does not *know*. The young man speaks at length this time but does not look in my direction, and his words are not pleasant. And then he turns to my husband, like someone preparing to say farewell: So goodbye Dr Jochanan, he says to my husband, and say goodbye to your wife for me. My husband gets up to accompany him to the door but the two go out together. My husband walks with him all the way down the stairs, and I hear their voices floating up from the courtyard.

—The young man's voice: It is said in the early and later commentaries . . . and my husband: And later commentaries—the end of all things. And the young man: But there is something in that, but not for us, not for us . . . My husband: Yes, there is something in that, but no joy. The young man: No, why would you say something like that? We'll see each other tomorrow . . . at morning prayers.—At morning prayers, my husband says. Before sunrise, in the snow, my husband says, for he is seized with enthusiasm. I imagine the young man's face with his cheekbones poking out from his wild beard, suddenly smiling with sharp white teeth, though he did not smile once the whole time he was in our home.

Holidays

Passover is close at hand. So close, and we have not had time to adjust to its coming. The days surrounding Purim[30] have barely passed and already another holiday is on the horizon, and I am still pondering the nature of this custom which forces people to pass so quickly from one holiday to the next while their souls are still distressed from the previous one. Holiday preparations are not for everyone, I think. But without a word my husband takes out a pair of long, sharpened scissors from the sideboard drawer, and begins cutting up sheets of paper which he bought yesterday, red paper. I see him from afar and I do not approach him. I have recently been assigned the job of checking map drawings in the new municipal press office. An order from Beersheba. I ask: Can I help? Even though . . . My husband answers: No. Without lifting his head. It is important to cut the papers along an imaginary straight line, and the scissors help him achieve this goal. My husband is engrossed in his work. And after that—the scotch tape. Packages of Milk Cow–brand milk chocolate, packaged in twos. Red ribbon around them, as sharp as a kitchen knife with no folds or wrinkles, and a flower for decoration. With no further ado those milk cows will go out in Purim gift packages to graze in others' pastures. And someone is knocking at the door. How few guests visit

30 A one-day Jewish holiday, falling exactly one month before the start of Passover, on which Jews celebrate their delivery from the wicked vizier Haman in the days of the Persian Empire.

our home lately. Like straw stubble at the end of a drought. Two little girls arrive. One is tall, wearing a blue garment over a white shirt. The garment is blue, and also her tights. She carries a package in her hand: a Purim gift package, she says, from the Pomerantz family.—Thank you, my husband says gleefully, thank you. Look, we got a Purim gift package! he calls to me. Here too paper fastened tightly with scotch tape. And her sister presses close to her. Thank you very much, girls, my husband says, and hurries to hand them a perfectly wrapped package of chocolate milk cows. Thank you! he cries again and waves his hand gently. And I return to my little room. Girls from the Diaspora . . . Perhaps they do not spend enough time in the sun. And their legs are always covered, I reflect, going out and then returning to kitchens of poverty, how pale they are . . . And I sit down on a low sofa with an equally low table before me, unsuited to my body structure, which is not short like the furniture. Music, also low, covers up the rustling of the red wrapping paper over which my husband labours, preparing his gift packages in the adjoining room. And I try to concentrate. Here: The order from Sha'ar Hanegev[31] finally arrived. From this date . . . year . . . Beersheba region 538/6. How wonderful is the sound of these names, calling me out.

But my husband does not hasten in his work. He has bought twenty bars of chocolate and prepared ten Purim gift packages by himself. He will request the son

31 'The Gate of the South', a settlement in the south of Israel.

of Shmulik the chef to distribute them among his acquaintances, and will pay him his wages in cash. For it is not proper for someone who is childless to distribute his Purim gift packages himself in order to save the delivery fee. And the cows are going out to pasture, my husband thinks, for he has gotten into a frivolous mood as required by the holiday. Children will rejoice over them, and parents will shake their heads as if they understand and agree: That fellow has strange ways . . . the parents will say, but what of it? He is trying, he is a good man, it's just that his lot is bitter because God has sent him a strange wife . . .

From Purim to Passover is only thirty days, but what demanding days they are. And I already know that there is no hope. No hope at all in this case. My husband carefully opens a narrow metal box, stamped with metal strips, and cautiously pulls out a silvery sheet, and then another one. It is needed to wrap the entire kitchen, marble counters, work surfaces on both sides of the sink, gas burners and baking oven, for they are also called work surfaces. They will be covered for seven or eight days, and the gas burners will be wrapped on both sides, front and back, and taped down at the edges. The aluminium foil is pliable and will not move once it is put in place, and the rest will be held down with scotch tape. And again my husband removes the long scissors from the sideboard drawer. This time he will prepare pieces of scotch tape ahead of time, and stick them to the work surfaces which have not yet been covered with sheets of aluminium foil, ready to use. How many narrow metal boxes fill our house then, and how many sheets of aluminium foil are rolled up in them. And now their numbers have shrunk, but they are still at risk of being used and reused. For some time I am placed in charge of peeling the scotch tape off the open surfaces, and then we switch. My husband busies himself tearing off strips of scotch tape and I wrap and cover, and this time he accepts my help and does not turn me away. The work progresses but not rapidly enough. The strips of scotch tape refuse to obey, and sometimes unstick themselves from the exposed surfaces. More than once they curl up and become entangled. During this whole process my husband is battling crumbs of leaven which he does not see but whose presence he assumes based on the testimony of law books and prayers. My husband goes out to wash his hands, because splinters of metal are stuck in the skin of his hands and have penetrated the upper layer of skin which is called the epidermis. When he returns, hours of work are already behind us and the holiday is near, and we have yet to prepare ourselves anything to eat.

In the German Colony we find ourselves a small grocery store which is open, and drag ourselves there. A man and his wife. In my hand is a bag of baked pita bread found in a corner of the bare bread shelf. The storekeeper hands it to me with a cold stare. Despite the monetary profit involved, Judaism is more important.

How these two are burning to fill their house with leaven on Passover, and the rest of the Jews are removing leaven from their souls, he thought. The storekeeper's thoughts do not please me, but we pay for the package and return home before that nebulous time when eating leaven will become forbidden but eating special Passover foods will also still be forbidden. And I do not say that I am hungry, in order not to spoil my husband's mood, lest he think that his wife cannot bear a few hunger pangs while exalted people do not complain even while being burnt at the stake for the sake of sanctifying God's name.

A man and wife are standing on the balcony of their flat. The April sun is shining, and pale paper cups are in their hands. A bottle of orange juice and a small plate of pita bread, over which they are leaning. I am bending down, lest the crumbs fall beyond the margins of the small plastic plate, of a pure sky-blue colour. We eat in a hurry, like the Israelites in their day. Their hurry was such that they did not have time to bake their bread properly. And the Oriental pita is a type of bread that has also not been baked properly, but for a different reason, and we eat our fill and drink from the bottle, and also drink from paper cups. And my husband bends down and reaches towards a corner of the balcony where earlier that day he placed a folded black plastic bag, now destined to receive the unfinished remains of the food we have eaten, and the paper cups we have drunk from and the empty juice bottle. And my husband takes the black bag in one hand, a trowel in the other, and goes down to the courtyard, where he rapidly digs a hole to hold the bag and all its contents, and covers up the hole with a little dirt. Our flat, meanwhile, is left leaven-free. And thus our flat is cleaned of all crumbs of leaven and all the kitchen appliances are covered in aluminium foil, except for the refrigerator, for which we did not have enough foil to wrap the entire exterior, and my husband took a single strip of foil and covered just the handle of the refrigerator, for it will be touched by human hands, and human hands are greasy. And all that remains to be done is to bathe ourselves, and from this one can conclude that everything is ready.

Before dark, we make our way to the hotel. For my husband has bought us tickets for a communal Passover Seder[32] at the Moriah Hotel. And we arrive early, for my husband has hurried me, lest we be late. We have dressed in our best clothes, and we choose a roundabout way and enjoy the leisurely walk that we have earned after all our hard work, and we relax. And here on the right, next to the low hill, I see the old leper colony, and a single light burns there. And I tell myself that the guard of the old leper colony is celebrating the holiday in his room, and he is not going out like we are to make friends with strangers. And I rejoice to myself.

32 The ceremonial meal on the first evening of the Passover holiday, at which Jews retell the story of the Exodus from Egypt.

People are sitting in family groups at long tables in the hotel dining room, and we are a family too, and we join another family, few in members like us, a man and wife sitting across the table from us.—I will go wash my hands, I say aloud, and then I will be ready for the reading and the meal. And I go to the washroom, and on my way back to my seat I pass the Lichtenstein family, with all their relatives and children and sons-in-law, and they occupy three long tables with waiters standing ready to serve them, and the mother of the family sits at the table next to her oldest son-in-law who is leaning on a cushion, and her husband is missing. For the news has spread that her husband has an incurable illness which struck him the previous winter, and he is lying in a sickroom at Mount Scopus Hospital and he does not recognize any of his acquaintances, for he has lost the sharp judgement which had brought him so far. And his wife has become the head of the family out of sorrow, and she is surrounded by grandchildren and great-grandchildren and her many daughters, and one of her sons-in-law approaches her to serve her: Perhaps, Mother, you would like a cup of tea before the Seder? And the other sons-in-law hush him: Before the Seder! That's not our custom! And the woman, Madam Lichtenstein, calms her sons-in-law: Enough, she says. And then: I do not need anything. We have everything here. And on her dress is a white-gold bird set with diamond chips which sparkle at me from afar. And I move on from there and approach the poor diners' area, among them former members of a religious kibbutz[33] who left their kibbutz, and their families abandoned them for that and no longer invite them to their former home, and also a few girls from the neighbouring girls' high school, who are boarding there because they have no parents to look after them, and the Szold Institute[34] pays for their holiday meals and for their rooms here. And I pass them by and approach our table and sit down next to my husband, and he raises his eyes to me and says: Where have you been? and I do not say a word. And I look and see our neighbours at the table, a young man and his wife, and fate has not treated them too shabbily. The large young man occupies the seat of an elevated wheelchair, and his head is resting on an appliance attached to it and he is inclined slightly upwards, and his young wife, though she does not move about in a wheelchair, has limbs which are limp and as short as a baby's. And the young man, when he wants to say something to his new wife—because the couple is only recently married, as they disclose to us later—has to speak with his head tilted towards the sky or the ceiling. But his wife jumps up and brings her ear as close as possible to his mouth. Did you say something, my dear? she asks, after moving her husband's wheelchair to and fro with her little hands, until

33 A settlement, originally agriculturally based, founded on socialist philosophy, in which all the members share the property and run the community jointly.

34 A non-profit organization founded in 1941 to support education and social service.

he is comfortably seated at the table. During the meal, she wipes his mouth and feeds him and herself alternately until they appear to me as one person who is entirely self-sufficient and is not interested in all the fruits of the world. And now the waitress arrives to ask if we are enjoying the food up to now, and if we would like to continue as we have begun, or perhaps, if we are not carnivores, they will serve us a meat substitute. And the couple next to us answers quickly: we are vegetarians, and my husband says: I am a carnivore. And I do not know what to say, and I also want to commit to vegetarianism forever, and I say: From this moment on, I am a vegetarian. And my husband looks at me severely, for that is not done where we come from, a Jew refraining from eating meat at holiday meals and particularly during Passover, and a married woman separating herself from her husband on this matter, and he is furious. But in comparison with me, he feels that his righteousness has increased.

And the couple next to us busies themselves opening a bag they have brought with them, and withdrawing from it a beautiful apple, and the woman with the baby's arms peels it delicately, divides it into four equal slices, and holds them out to us, like my husband did one summer evening when we were first married, when he gently held out the slices of fruit to me, and she serves all of us.

Ritual Bath and Wedding

And now the wedding, scheduled for Tuesday evening. Three days before it, we find ourselves walking to the ritual bath, for my husband has insisted that the grace of Judaism will shine on our wedding day. We find a ritual bathhouse near our home, a twenty- or twenty-five-minute walk away, open to the public at all hours of the day and night as a sort of public aid station, located in one of the alleyways leading off the eastern end of Palmach Street. And I walk next to my husband, who has asked to accompany me, relying on the verse 'helpmate . . . etc.' which he has called on to strengthen the connection between a married couple. The ritual bathhouse is like a bathhouse from bygone days. One enters the building after a short walk down a flagstone path lined with dense vegetation which in the dusk looks like a narrow tropical forest, into which the rays of the setting sun scarcely penetrate. When we reach the entrance, my husband stops and says: No further. This place is not for me but, rather, for the women examiners in the women's section. And you will wait for me here? I ask, for I do not yet know his ways.— Of course, he answers, I will wait and wait, as long as necessary. My husband answers in military style because he is in a good mood, and I go in. I find a waiting room full of women. Some are walking to and fro to stretch their legs, others are seated on benches and chairs and only their lips are moving and their voices are silent, and they are reading small books of Psalms or weekday prayer books, for today is not a holiday, and they are waiting for their names to be called by the clerk, signifying that their turn to immerse themselves has arrived, and I also register in the clerk's book and wait for my name to be called. Time passes and the air does not stir, but a spirit of tranquillity reigns over those waiting there. And two women begin to converse among themselves and I overhear them, for they live next door to each other and they have many matters to discuss.

They are discussing the dresses that they need to sew for themselves to prepare for the many upcoming weddings, may they be for good luck, and the holiday finery which they will buy their children in honour of the weddings and other celebrations also coming up, for these events are already almost upon them. And one speaks of her husband who does not allow her to sew on Saturday nights after the Sabbath goes out, and all the rest of the week she is laden with work, and when evening arrives she drops down on a pile of bedding and falls asleep, and the day of the celebration is approaching and there is still no dress. And I listen, and the calm that has fallen on me lulls me to sleep while hearing these words. But I cannot rest completely, for I hear my husband's footsteps as he paces outside, and there is no rest in his footsteps. And now the clerk's call is heard in the room, and I approach and enter the bathing room. Where is the immersion attendant? I wonder. For I have encountered such a being in the

Hebrew language, but I have never seen a real live one outside of the words, and except for a woman who is swathed head to toe in rough cotton garments and a sort of turban on her head, struggling to clean the railing leading into the immersion pool, I have seen no other living soul there, and I do not realize that I am looking at the immersion attendant, until she looks up at me and asks me my age and how many years I have been alive on this earth, and I say thirty-five years, and I still do not know why she wants to know. And the immersion attendant commands me to remove my clothes and place them in one of the cubbies along the walls, and to let her know when I have completed this task. And thus, while she is still dressed and her entire body is covered except for an opening for her face—even her hands are covered by rubber gloves, for most of her work is done under water—and I am entirely without clothes, she instructs me to descend the stairs until I reach the bottom of the pool, and I am still clutching the metal railing which guided me down. And I already stand there wrapped only in my hair, my head and shoulders above water, and the attendant encourages me: Keep going down! Keep going down! But her voice is severe. It sounds to me like the voice of a seal trainer, and now I am in the water up to my neck, and the attendant tells me to continue walking on the bottom of the pool down to the point where a strip of cloth hangs across the pool, bearing the word DANGER written in large letters. And I take one or two more steps, and now the water reaches my mouth, and I no longer feel air coming into my mouth and I lose consciousness because quantities of water wash over my lips and enter my mouth, and I barely manage to thrust one of my hands out of the water to signal to the attendant that I am drowning.—And now stand, the attendant says, and there is nothing next to me to hold on to and no one to hear her words except me, for there is no one in the place except the two of us, and all her words are directed at me. And there is no railing or supporting wall next to me. In the whole world, there is just me and the attendant and my husband's faraway steps. Now stand! the attendant says, and now go under! Eyes down! Bend down more and more! I take my life in my hands, for standing in the heart of the mighty waters makes me dizzy. And I lower my head, cross my arms over my chest, immerse myself to the depths and then come up.—No good! the attendant calls. No good at all! Your hair was floating on the surface of the water! Do it all again! I wonder why she has not told me earlier to pin my hair close to my head with some kind of kerchief, and I must immerse myself again, and again a hair from my head floats on the surface and my immersion is not proper. And I repeat this three more times and three more times my immersion is declared not proper, and only the fourth time the attendant says: Enough! So be it . . . And her tone softens a little. And immediately I forgive her in my heart.

The attendant hands me a large towel and a yellow plastic rectangle. This I am to give the clerk on the way out to signify that my immersion has been completed.—And the secretary will give you a certification for the Rabbinate, the attendant says.

When I come out, there are still women sitting in the waiting room. My hair is wet, like theirs, only they have increased in number. The two women who sewed themselves dresses for weddings are no longer there. I think that this ritual bathhouse is probably constructed with many sections, with an attendant for each cell, and I feel uncomfortable because I do not know how I will look to my husband with my wet hair, and after a long evening of waiting. I go out into the street air by the entrance where I came in many hours ago. The broad-leafed plants are still there like before and the flavour of a distant tropical forest rests among them. But the day is over. The air carries the chill of approaching night and the light is gone. I do not see my husband. Apparently he has lost patience and left. Or perhaps he is sitting at home and awaiting my return, and something of his impatience clings to me, mixed with a sense of let-down, and cheerlessly I trace his footsteps home.

But as the wedding preparations picked up speed, my husband diligently supervised the many details. It was he who chose the location for the wedding canopy and investigated the quality of the hall where the wedding meal would be served, and who would be invited to the meal, and the quality of the dishes served to the guests, course after course, and what would each course be called, and what type of paper would the menu be written on, and what font it would be printed in, whether tall letters or short, round ones, and what exactly does that symbolize. And my husband busied himself with all this, and also expressed interest in the quality of the fish to be served to the guests, and if it was caught properly in the depths of the North Sea, while he insisted and demanded again as he had when he first arrived at the place, and laid his requests before the hotel's guest manager, and wondered if his request had been forgotten, like the rest of his requests and demands had been forgotten, and the fish was caught wherever and its flesh bought in the supermarket next door, where it was dumped in the same barrel with sardines and sprats from cans, giving off a strange odour. My husband dealt with all these issues in his own way. And paid for everything with his own money, until I began to see myself as a guest at my own wedding, while my husband said to himself: Now she has become a guest at her own wedding. And my husband travelled to Tel Aviv with me to buy a suitable wedding dress. And we wandered in and out of stores and did not find a suitable garment. My husband grew weary but I was not yet tired, and he became annoyed at this, for he said to himself: On all other days she lacks energy and strength of will. She even avoids hard work. And he recalled how I had taped the sheets of aluminium foil to the kitchen work surfaces before Passover with an uncertain hand, and he said: she is even lazy, but he said nothing to me, just found a small kosher restaurant along the way and ordered us steaming sausages in sauerkraut and a vegetable salad with mayonnaise. We ate our fill, and only when we left the restaurant did we find a suitable clothing store. It was right around the corner. I bought myself a skirt and blouse and a white vest to go with the blouse. And the blouse fit me tightly at the waist, and the saleswoman dressed me and stroked the fabric of the blouse, sliding over it a bit, and did the same to the fabric of the skirt, and my husband's face darkened to the point where he commented as we left: She is a lesbian and she is lusting for you, and directed his words to the saleswoman at the clothing store, but I rejoiced over the clothes I had bought, and from the wedding day I do not remember much, except that I wore my new clothes, and the Eybeschutz family came, Israel and his wife Miriam, our neighbours from the upper floor, and blind Johaness and his wife who had returned from France. But old Shapira did not come because it was difficult for him to move about. And three of my relatives arrived from Tel Aviv, as well as my husband's acquaintance from Hadera who was ordained in the Rabbinate, with his wife, and several people from the Swedish community whom I had never met before, and I do not clearly remember anything that took place under the wedding canopy, the way I remember what happened under others' wedding canopies, which I had observed in the past without difficulty, whereas placing the ring on my finger 'according to the laws of Moses and Israel' I did not remember at all, the memory fading entirely the more I tried to remember, and the matter was forgotten immediately as though it had never happened. A man came up to me after the wedding ceremony and said: This man you have married, he is an extraordinary person. And he stressed the word 'extraordinary' in a strange way, and I did not know if he meant it for good or for evil. I waited a little and he did not add anything more, and I asked him, Who are you? Are you a friend of his?

He said: Pearls and dust, pearls and dust, and he was still talking about my husband as though he knew him well.

—And you, who are you?

—I am a friend, from Akko.

And he left. I called after him: Pearls and dust . . . Thank you, I will remember that.

He was tall and lean as he walked and he did not turn to face me again. He looked to me like a partisan who fought the Germans in Russian forests. But that was not possible.

The dining room where the wedding feast took place was on the top floor of the hotel, facing East Jerusalem. The golden dome of the mosque on the Temple Mount looked so close, and lights of Jerusalem below it. It was already evening, and a kind of tranquillity, tranquillity everywhere. My husband withdrew a carefully folded piece of white paper from his shirt pocket, and opened it to reveal a delicately sketched map showing the dining table and the guests' places around it, in bird's eye view like all maps, and each guest's name was marked at the place my husband had assigned to him on the map before he put it on paper, when it was still just in his imagination. And as the guests approached, my husband marked each guest's seat and sometimes it did not go smoothly, for not all the guests were practised at reading such symbols, and now one of my husband's friends, who had arrived in Israel together with him on the same voyage, moved one of the chairs intended for another guest. I am just making myself a place next to her, she said, please, sit here, Mrs Tobias. She wanted to make me happy, and therefore called me by my new name, but my husband just wrung his hands helplessly, saying: What have you done to me? For she had disturbed the coordination between chairs and guests' names, and the actual order and the planned order no longer matched, and everything was spoilt.

But a few flowers were scattered on the table, and they lent a pleasant feeling to the place, and the windows of the room were long and narrow and close together so that the view of the dark city with its lights was like a wonderful painting. And Israel Eybeschutz rapped on his empty wine glass with a small fork to signal that he wanted to bless the guests. And he blessed God first, and then all of us, opening with the words: Dear friends, this morning I prayed hastily at the Western Wall. I ran there together with my son, who received a long weekend's vacation from Gush Katif. We ran there side by side, and to tell the truth, we walked. But with energetic steps. They were almost running steps. We were in such a hurry to pray there. I do not know what my son was thinking at that time, but I was thinking of you, and your good hearts, and all of us that have made the effort to come here to rejoice with our friend and be blessed by the joy of his marriage to the one his heart has chosen . . . Three times during the meal and between the courses, Israel Eybeschutz asked permission to speak, and three times he set his crystal wine glass vibrating with a delicate ring. And the other two times he also blessed the host and hostess—for thus he saw us—that they should merit to build a Jewish home in accordance with God's laws. Israel Eybeschutz's words washed grace and kindness over the guests, and when the wedding feast was over and the guests turned to leave, blessing us a second time, and the waiters who had worked so hard around us began clearing the remaining dishes from the table, and even I, holding two bags in my hands, moved towards the entrance of the hall, I saw from some distance away one of the waiters, a handsome lad with an alert look in his slanted eyes, and he had worked hard for us during the meal, and now he came up to my husband with words of parting, and my husband extended his hand. And the lad brought my husband's hand up to his lips and kissed it, saying: 'Bless me, sir.'

'Pictures of Married Life'

Thus days passed. Were they many? I do not remember. I wander the streets of the city. Stores that I used to frequent—I no longer enter them. Even bookstores have ceased to draw me. Once my husband returned home with a child's teddy bear, perhaps a conciliatory gift, and I smiled weakly; I am no longer a child . . . I did not grace my husband with my gaze. Let him go and complain about that. In those days he would visit Shapira frequently in the evenings, and something of that old man's gait infected him. I felt it without him saying a word. I thought: what makes Old Shapira cast such a jaundiced eye on our marriage, but he was careful of my husband's honour and would not say anything explicitly, and perhaps he believed that this way his words would sink in deeper. Not directly, not with a trumpet blast would the walls come down, but, rather, by way of the forgotten moat. From the depths they would crumble.

Shapira did not like my appearance. Once my husband brought me to his house. For he was not at our wedding, and why would it not be appropriate for him to see the bride? During the conversation he mentioned the laws defining where one can carry objects on the Sabbath, laws which Jerusalemites are careful to observe, not like those who live in Tel Aviv. I said: Every town has its own character. And with that his face darkened towards me: not every town with its own character, but one law for everyone, and it is found in our holy Torah. After that, I could no longer please him. And one of the yeshiva students who was helping him, for it was the Sabbath day, asked whether we would drink tea or perhaps we would agree to eat from a pitcher of cooked fruit compote prepared by Mr Shapira's daughter Miriam. I said: No, we don't need anything. Thank you. And my husband said: Fruit soup—let's have some, for he liked to disagree with me. And Shapira and my husband ate fruit soup and took little sips to prolong their pleasure, and I did not touch it. I got up and looked at the rows of books on the bookshelves. And I pulled out *The Treasury of Jewish Books*, which is a dictionary for all the books of the far-flung Jewish diaspora, new and old. It was published in Vilna in the year of the new emperor's birth, and I paged through it, and there was also *The Book of the Covenant* by Esh Horowitz, and a supplementary book with 'proverbs and parables' and a book of prologues and introductions to various books, and Agor's ancient parables. And I sunk into vacant musings, and Shapira and my husband were discussing the harsh punishment that befell Korach and his sons and grandsons and all his gang.

And as we were walking home, quite soon after we set out, my husband announced: I did not know how much aggression you have in you. And added: A lot of aggression . . . And I understood that I have not found favour in his friend Shapira's eyes. We returned home and I tried to find comfort in the books on our bookshelves, for I said to myself, perhaps I will find *The*

Treasury of Jewish Books here too and it will give me strength. Meanwhile, I found *Steppenwolf* and the rest of the books by Hermann Hesse, and I did not see any rhyme or reason in them. But I saw in them something else, for their first and last pages, as well as the margins of the inner pages, were covered with dense handwriting, as though the letters were climbing on top of each other. The writing was in German, and some in English and French. And I learnt that the niece Rita wrote those words and even signed her name more than once, as though to say: I am here. And here—my thoughts. And they seemed to me like wet lambs asking to be let into the electric dryer to dry off and come out refreshed and warm, and their fragrance is like that of the words within the books where the niece Rita's words linger to return and receive their fragrance. And I understand that Rita also lived in this flat before me and she too passed by these books. To find in them something she hoped for, and when she gave up hope—she wrote what she wrote in them, and left and returned to her home across the sea, for her soul did not find peace in Jerusalem.

And my husband said: It's time to make a place for you in our flat, Naomi. And the way he spoke that word 'our' touched my heart, for he shared his home with me equally. At that time, my husband collected all the remaining clothing belonging to Sonia, the Russian woman, since she had not come to our house to collect them and therefore apparently no longer wanted them. And my husband collected all the clothing and also

RACHEL SHIHOR | 104

packed up the silvery sneakers, and piled everything into a green suitcase and ordered a taxi to bring the baggage to Sonia's house. And Sonia had returned from living with the old man whom she had cared for in the past. And when my husband had put down the suitcase, leaning against the outside of the old man's flat door, in one of the tall buildings in Baka'a, and the taxi driver who brought my husband was waiting for him near the building for my husband had said, I will be right back, and Sonia heard the rustle of the suitcase moving, with its metal rings to guard its contents, and she opened the door and grabbed the suitcase with one hand while reaching out with the other towards my husband's buttoned-up coat, pulling him inside. And the taxi driver waited impatiently and did not refrain from honking his horn several times, until he gave up on taking him back and said once more to himself that you can't rely on Jews and went on his way.

And my husband returned home in the evening and said: I have freed up two big drawers for you. I filled the drawers with all my possessions and there was still not enough room for them all. And my husband started going through his files, in order to get rid of any unneeded documents and thereby free up more space for my possessions. And I knew this task would take a long time due to my husband's love of numbers and lists, for he usually became absorbed in reading them whenever he came across them, and often would recalculate the order of the previous numbers to check if something was left out or perhaps added to the original list. And I suggested that perhaps we could buy an additional closet for our flat.—And where will we put it? my husband asked, his mood soured, the flat is too small . . . —In the small room, I said, I thought of this a few days ago, the eastern wall of the small room is almost completely free.—The eastern wall . . . the eastern wall . . . my husband said, and still he went out and came back with a rolled-up measuring tape in his hand. He measured one side and wrote it in a notebook, and then measured the height of the wall and its depth, and not to forget the depth, he said, and took out the notebook again. In doing so his gaze brushed the small coffee table standing there, leaning against the eastern wall with its surface tilted towards me. The table was an object from his former home, and it arrived in Israel in the lift together with all the other household effects. But while all the other household objects arrived unharmed, the coffee table was damaged during the journey and its surface became warped. That is to say: it leant towards the left and could no longer support any weight. And my husband's glance fell on the damaged table and he thought to himself: I should call a carpenter to fix that table, but he did not say anything out loud, and as he was measuring the eastern wall a second time to make sure that there was no error in the first measurement, he understood that his soul would find no peace, and he would not be able to take up some new activity until he fixed what was damaged in the old things, and that meant he would need to take

care of fixing the coffee table before he could take on
the task of purchasing a new closet. So he decided to
call a carpenter to the house. The carpenter would fix
the coffee table and it would cease leaning to the left,
and then he would be free to make a closet for my
clothing and other possessions.

The carpenter was scheduled to arrive early in the
morning, and my husband had laboured to straighten
up the flat before his arrival lest he decide that we lived
in a dirty flat like farm animals. Thus spoke my husband, for he loved to express himself in extremes. And
I thought about farm animals and how we are like them,
in that we inhale and exhale, and also perspire and
excrete all the other things that bodies need to excrete,
and we eat and drink like them, and therefore, how similar we are to animals, whether domesticated or wild
. . . but the carpenter was due to arrive any minute and
there was no time for wandering thoughts. My husband
urged me to gather up all folders containing important
papers, travel documents or money, and place them in
the closet in the second room, where the carpenter
would not be working, and my husband would lock the
closet, because carpenters were no different from the
rest of humanity, and the imagination of man's heart is
evil, etc.,[35] and I did as he asked, and he was satisfied.

The carpenter fixed the coffee table and attached
its legs solidly with wood glue whose odour lingered

35 Genesis 8:21: ' . . . for the imagination of man's heart is evil
from his youth . . . '

in the house for several days after he had finished his work and gone, and the smell of wood glue was pleasant to me in those days, and the carpenter warned my husband not to stand the coffee table immediately on its freshly glued legs, until the glue dried and was absorbed into the wood. Rather, he told my husband to turn the table upside down with its legs pointing up. The carpenter did not specify how long the table should remain in this temporary position, before it could be turned over again and returned to its habitual place. After the carpenter left, I picked up an old broom and swept up the wood shavings which had curled up on the floors after his labour, and my husband took the coffee table and placed it upside down on the couch in the small room, which was my regular spot in those days. And I squeezed myself onto the couch next to the upside-down table, and it did not leave me much space, but I could still manage to sit on the couch and do my work like before. Thus days passed and my work inched along, and I said to myself: But I will not get angry. And my friend Michal from Tel Aviv came to visit me, for she had an appointment with a doctor in Jerusalem. She sat with me in the little room and we crowded together there on the couch, and then I got up and went into the kitchen to make us coffee. When I returned with a tray in my hands, bearing two cups of hot coffee and a plate of cookies, I saw that the upside down coffee table had been removed from its place on the couch, and my friend had stood it on its legs and was pointing to it, saying: Here, put the tray here. And we sat on the couch and drank and ate cookies, and we placed our tray on the formerly sloping coffee table, and the tray did not move even a hair's breadth out of place. Thus nothing more stood in the way of purchasing the closet for me. And I got back my spacious seating accommodations.

Before winter was out, we went looking for a furniture store in the centre of town. During that winter, we could not say: Now it's snowing again, or even: Now it's snowing. The days were clear and dry, though not warm. A dry wind brought tears to my eyes and made my lips crack. We wandered from the centre outwards towards the periphery, and did not find ourselves a furniture store. You won't find a furniture store here, I said to myself, but you will find a carpentry studio, for we had reached a district populated by small businesses and studios. There were no furniture stores here, though many of the studios featured collections of discarded furniture at their entrances, and the upholsterers—all men—spread thick fabrics on dismantled couches, attempting to subdue wayward steel springs and spread them with a colourful covering. Is there a carpenter here? my husband asked a worker in a grey vest. There are no carpenters here, the worker answered, attempting to straighten a leg of a couch whose springs still jutted out from beneath its fabric covering. The worker looked up and met my husband's eyes.—I am Saul the Upholsterer, said the upholsterer, and I did not know whether he was scorning my husband for his question or perhaps he liked my husband and therefore he divulged to him his name and his profession, and perhaps he was indifferent to all questions directed at him, and had only one stock answer which he had conceived once long ago, and my husband was silent. And from there we turned towards a dimly lit carpentry studio, pointed out to us by an old man selling lemonade from a wooden stall. From the start we had been seeking a large furniture store whose name—Weinberg and Sons—we knew, and my husband even remembered the store clearly but did not know where it was located. He asked passers-by where to find the store, and the people, most of them swathed in woollen scarves and gloves against the unpleasant dry wind, answered him that it was this way or that way, but not one of them gave precise directions, and perhaps did not even actually know where the store was located, but did not want to turn us away empty-handed, and thus we walked from the centre of the city to the periphery, all the way to the district of small studios, named for Rabbi Salant. At this point, we were ready to settle for any carpentry studio at all, and we had entirely forgotten the name of the store Weinberg and Sons. All we wanted was to find a carpentry studio, and not one of the multitude of upholstery studios surrounding us, with the smell of combed fabric hanging about them (despite the wind which whistled through them—for these workshops had no doors to be seen). The carpentry studio at whose entrance we finally stood, the one indicated by the lemonade seller, was

dimly lit and looked no different from the many upholstery studios, for it also lacked doors, and it welcomed
us inside in the manner of carpentry studios, and we
sat on a low wooden bench and waited until the owner
finished what he was doing and came over to us. And
my husband gave the owner our address and other
pertinent information, and we agreed that tomorrow a
carpenter's apprentice would come and take measure-
ments for the closet. Meanwhile, the clamorous
pounding of air hammers rang out from a distance and
we turned to go.

The nearby bus stop, its sign indicating that five or
six bus lines stopped there, was enveloped in smoke
which swallowed us up too. I covered my face with my
scarf for the odour of the tar-laden smoke was almost
unbearable, and my husband looked at me but I could
not see his eyes, and I listened to construction workers'
voices which, though coming to us from some distance
away, drowned out all other sounds except the air hammers' pounding.

The voice of worker A was heard: Water level!

The voice of worker B was heard: Bricks!

Worker A: Water level!

Worker B: Plaster trowel!

A: Hammer!

B: You're a nuisance!

A: Fresh plaster!

B: All gone!

A: Yellow block!

B: Aren't any.

My husband looked me in the face: we were still a mystery to each other.—They are working people, he said finally, and sighed. And even if it is not so pleasant to you, *they* must make a living. My husband searched my face for signs of displeasure, and suddenly the bus we had been waiting for pulled up, and it seemed like a miracle to me, like an envoy from a faraway land coming to carry us away from here, and we climbed aboard the bus.

In the following days, my husband returned later and later from synagogue. Sometimes the day would be almost over and he still had not returned. On other days, when it was already evening, he virtually snuck out of the flat, without saying goodbye when he left, and only the rattling of the lock was heard when he went out and came in, for sometimes my husband locked the door after himself when he left because he forgot that he was married and his wife was at home. Yet he went out to discuss his marriage with strangers. He did something similar on Thursday mornings, when the cleaning lady Sarah arrived at our home to clean his flat and he admired her knowledge of Hebrew, which was better than his since she was born here and had not arrived here from a foreign country, and even so it seemed to him something strange and wonderful, and every week in the centre of town he made a point of buying a bag full of cheese pastries which she particularly liked, and she would heat them up in the oven when she took her coffee break. And yet, she slipped his awareness when he went out on his morning errands, and he would lock the flat door after him, leaving Sarah the cleaning lady locked inside to do her work until my husband returned from his wanderings to rescue her, and he did not see anything wrong with this.

And once my husband slipped out of the house as he usually did in the evening, and forgot about me and locked the door after him, and I, I could not find a spare key for myself at that time. And I sat and waited. And now our neighbour from the third floor came knocking at the door, for she was missing black pepper for the dish she was making, and the whole Eybeschutz family pours pepper on any food which is not sweet. And Miriam Eybeschutz stood on the other side of the closed door and waited until the whole scene became humiliating. Finally I screwed up my courage, for I suddenly felt sorry for her, and I explained to her timidly, from the other side of the door, that my husband had not noticed that he locked the door because he is not used to . . . , and the rumour spread rapidly among all the tenants of the building, with the single exception of the secular neighbour, and they would watch me as I passed by and secretly nicknamed me 'the imprisoned neighbour', for I was branded with the mark of all prisoners, that if they are imprisoned, it is a sign that they must have done something evil and are being punished for it.

And then my husband's absences from the flat increased in frequency, and he started going out every evening. And even though he no longer locked the door after himself when he left, I could feel his absence, for the house fell quiet and I did not hear the sound of his footsteps as I used to, and only when he would return and avoid looking at me directly, as though ashamed, did I understand that he had found an advisor in his friend, the old Shapira, and that he was following his advice by making himself a stranger to me. And the wall between us grew higher. And Old Shapira's advice was the mortar which increased the height of the wall. And once my husband could not hold out any more and he said to me: Who are you? I said: What does your question mean, my friend? You know who I am. And he said that he did not know anything about me before we met, and he was so swept away with love for me, like mighty floodwaters, that he did not investigate anything about me, just looked at me all day and never ceased to see new visions.

—And I asked: And what have you discovered about me?

—And he said: That you are Lilith. Or one of the creatures of the underworld, and just dress yourself in a pleasant human appearance.

—Why would you say that? I asked, for I heard something like laughter in his voice.

—When we came back that day from the carpentry studio, as you will surely remember right away, we waited for a bus at the bus stop, but the bus was delayed.

—I remember. I will remember for a long time. And you, you didn't think of a taxi, at least so that . . . I also remember that there was no air to breathe.

—But the workers had air. And I would never take a taxi. You should have understood that.

—Yes, I said. I understood that.

—My husband said: That is not the issue.

—I asked: And what is the issue?

—My husband said: The issue is when you got on the bus.

—When I got on the bus?

—You did not pay for yourself, and afterwards I got on and paid for only one ticket because the driver said, As for the woman who just got on, it's OK. What does 'OK' mean? It was something sexual.

—OK, because I did pay, and before that the driver was joking. He was in a good mood and did not want to take money . . . The driver was talking nonsense. But that's not the issue.

—And my husband: That's not the issue. You're right.

—I asked: So what is it then?

—My husband said: So then, Shapira is advising me . . . It's possible for a Jew to get divorced.

—I asked: And what do the others say?

—My husband said: Others? I didn't ask any others.

—I said: You didn't ask the rabbi from Hadera?

—My husband said: Aryeh?

—I said: Yes, Aryeh. Aryeh who wanted to marry you without the government's knowledge . . .

—My husband said: Aryeh said, If worst comes to worst, divorce is not a disaster.

And for some time we did not talk about this matter. Days and perhaps weeks passed, and my husband began to feel a disquieting pain which repeatedly seized his body. It appeared when he urinated—the urine came out slowly, drop by drop, in fits and starts. And my husband would spend a long time in the bathroom, and once when he came out, he informed me that his urine was red. And we spoke of the matter, and the hostility between us faded, but the word 'divorce', ever since it was spoken then, a first and then a second time, did not fade. And I feared for my husband's health, but he reassured me, as though it was a known thing for men to have their kidneys fail sometimes, and I should not worry. Problems like this pass naturally. And perhaps it is an infection, he added.—But you need to get checked, I said.—Yes, I know I need to get checked, my husband said, I'm a doctor, after all.

And we went out one cloudy morning for a check-up which had been scheduled for my husband at Hadassah Hospital which is built on a hill, surrounded by hills with its parking lots in their shadow, and residents of this country consult with its doctors about every evil, and residents of neighbouring countries as well, who do not like us, also come for consultation and hospitalization. My husband had an appointment at ten o'clock to be examined by one of the department doctors, and we set out while it was still daylight. And my husband quickened his pace and his stride was firm, not like an invalid's stride, while my steps faltered. Look, we have switched places in the world, I said to myself, and my husband has become the healthy one while I am the invalid. And we had to walk a long way to get to the bus stop, whose location I did not know, for I did not know the life of this city nor its habits very well. And en route to the bus stop we passed an elegant old-age residence with a golden fence climbing up to the top of the hilly street and even beyond. When we reached the entrance to the residence, my husband suddenly quickened his pace, and the sun emerged from behind a cloud and its rays struck the painted metal of the fence, making it glow. And the glow swallowed up the image of my husband. In another moment my husband disappeared from my sight, for he broke into a run as he passed the corner of the building. When he had disappeared I said to myself, I will leave him and return to my home. Why should I spend all my strength running after a crazy person? But my heart would not let me, and I knew that the pain in his body was keeping him awake at night. And I continued walking, my strength almost spent, and I did not quicken my pace any more, saying, Whatever will be, will be. It is not for me to control things. And I continued to walk the length of the street with the golden fence, and the street went uphill like Jerusalem streets do, sometimes steeply, for the city is not built on a flat plain like Tel Aviv but, rather, on a rocky mountain. And just as I passed the end of the street and my legs carried me to the right, I saw my husband standing at the bus stop, smiling at me, and I did not know what to say.

We came to the clinic and found a crowd densely packed around the clinic doors and the eternally closed doors of the doctors' offices, and some of them crouched on wooden benches, and at the end of the corridor was a drinking fountain and a sullen nurse coming out and commanding the crowd, in the name of the doctors, to drink a lot before their examination so that it would come out well, even if they were incurably ill. And the line was long, and many of those waiting in line had come furnished with mandarin oranges, which are easy to peel and to carry among their other paraphernalia. And the sounds of peeling resonated in the hall, and the air was thick with the sweet fragrance of citrus. But the faces of those waiting showed the tension of anticipation. I also stood in line, holding an empty cup in my hands, and watched the faces of the passers-by. I saw a mother leaning against one of the walls, holding her son in her arms, her body swathed in the garments of our neighbours from nearby Bethlehem. And I remembered that among my other trappings I had a whistle that a bus driver once gave me when we returned together from the carpentry studio, and the driver pretended to refuse my payment and joked around, wanting just for once to change the order of things, and give a passenger something of his rather than always receiving something, and he gave me a small driver's whistle that he had with him, and I accepted it and did not tell my husband. And he, who got on after me, saw and did not see, but resented me for it. And now I found that very whistle in my bag, as handsome and sparkling as ever, and I held it out to a child. And the child smiled at me, openmouthed, and all his teeth were perfect. And afterwards I sat down and gave the filled cup of water to my husband and he drank.

It was almost our turn, and hours of sitting in the corridor had passed over us. And now I saw a friend whom I knew from my former job working for Davidov the architect. She was accompanied by a companion, and I remembered that even back then she had to frequent this clinic at regular intervals. We rejoiced at our unexpected meeting, and my friend turned and said to her companion: I'd like to introduce you to Naomi. And we smiled, shook hands and exchanged pleasant greetings, and I turned my head to the left so I could introduce my husband, but my husband was no longer where he had been sitting before, and I did not know where he had gone, and our neighbours on the bench who, out of sheer boredom, transformed all the waiting patients into stage actors, and followed all their movements precisely, informed me with a wave of a hand that my husband had been called into the examination room and left his place on the bench, for they were too lazy to spell out the information in words. And the matter distressed me greatly but I did not say anything to my friend and her companion, for I was careful to preserve my husband's honour and my honour in their eyes. But my husband still did not return from the examination room, and my earlier resentment faded away, and apprehension pierced my heart, and I said farewell to my friend and went out to look for him. And I walked to the end of the corridor and did not find him, and there was one door standing open, leading to the inner chambers. A long time had passed since my husband was called inside and I had no news of him, and my dread was swelling with every passing moment, and I nudged the door open slightly and went in.

It turned out to be a ward of treatment rooms, and the room doors were partially or fully open, and they all faced a single common lobby. And they also faced each other, for between them were rooms which passed into other rooms and hallways and faraway lobbies, and the only thing missing was an opening to the outside. And I entered one of the rooms which was shrouded in darkness, for daylight had already faded, and the room was long and wide like a convention hall, and there was a bed at the end of it. I approached the bed to see who was lying in it, and it was not my husband but a woman at the end of her life, her face as white as plaster. And I wended my way from room to room and there was no one there except patients whom I did not know. And each room held no more than a single patient, and I did not know whether it was a place for people to recover, or to be examined by doctors and their instruments, or to die with nothing left to be done. And I had almost given up in despair when I suddenly found my husband in one of those rooms, and he was lying at the end of the room on a raised bed, and his face was conveying something, and the room was neither large nor small.—Jochanan, I said in panic, coming up close to him, How are you? Who examined you? I spoke quietly, so as not to shatter the tranquillity of the patient, the place, and everyone in it, and my husband signalled with his hand that I should leave, as though he was pushing me away and was not glad I had come.

And some days passed, and my husband recovered from his illness, and nothing changed, and our fate was determined: that we would live side by side while the boat that bore us was sinking, and we ourselves were the sinking boat, and we carried its name. And neither of us dared to bring up these things until they came up of their own accord, clear and simple. And I had to empty out a travelling bag and fill it with shoes and clothes, folded in such a way that they would not wrinkle, and my husband watched as though he did not understand but actually everything was agreed between us. I will go away for one or two days, perhaps longer. And each of us will remain in his loneliness and his thoughts day and night. And it seemed to me the right thing to do, and I did not feel the pain of parting, for it was not a true parting.

And my husband called a taxi and walked me out, and I carried the travelling bag. And we passed by Old Shapira's house, now dull because few sought him out any more since he left his government job and was not restoring any new graves of righteous people, and we passed the shady bench under the leafy tree, and the youth who had lost a leg sat under it, trying to attach a skateboard to his single leg. And we mounted the stone steps to the road joining the two neighbourhoods, and a taxi was standing there with its engine running. I went up to my husband and he hugged me. For a moment he stroked my hair and buried his head in my shoulder, and when he pulled away I saw that his face was awash with tears. He said only: You are my soulmate. And I was struck dumb. I did not know anything.

PART TWO

Trip to Poland

I returned to Tel Aviv, carrying the thoughts with me. Those days felt like a school holiday from when I was a girl. As for my husband, each evening, while I was still speaking with him in my mind, he would call me on the telephone. Once, I told him that I was going out to a party at Davidov's, my former boss, celebrating the publication of his book on multi-storey buildings in the Land of Israel, and he did not take it amiss. It was as though it was natural for me to spend my time in pleasant pursuits while he was stuck alone with few visitors.—But did he not choose that way of life, and he does not see it as terrible, and why should you feel sorry for him? I told myself then, and I did not know if it was the separation between us, or anticipating the joy of meeting again, which strengthened my heart. And on one of those days, my husband told me of his plans to travel to Poland, and it was as if he was saying: Come with me. In his heart he was actually saying: I will test her again and see how I will proceed from there. But I thought that my husband was calling me to return to him.

We travelled to Poland. We flew to a country which scarcely differed from the country we had left. In what did it differ? In the museums which housed its treasures which were dear to the heart of the country's citizens, for those treasures belonged to the people no less than their houses and their little cars and their children, and included knights' armour from the tenth and twelfth centuries, and these were stored in cool cellars; in the castles of the kings who once ruled the country without end, and all of Polish history is made up of their names; and also in the highly praised university which boasts of its learned student, Nicolaus Copernicus, in these things it differed, and I will say more of these later. And in what way was it similar? In the pride of its people for simply belonging to that country; in their admiration for the wretched history which tags along with them; in their love for the poets who wrote longingly of their homeland from exile; in being a green country along the highways and byways, green and tedious; in the aged ornamentation clinging to it, marked with poverty and enervation.

From the Warsaw airport we travel as far as Cracow, and there, too, no shade is to be found, and the temperature stands at thirty-eight degrees Celsius. All the newspapers in the city announce this fact. I look at my husband's face—no change. Now we are living in a hotel—and again no change. At breakfast—my husband examines me with his gaze lest I fail, perhaps my manners will not meet the local requirements, perhaps I ordered milk for my coffee and the waiter brought me water instead, and my husband is waiting to see if I will get angry. And we walk to the city entrance to see the old market and the old city which everyone praises. We are like tourists. And to the head of the city wall, where peddlers spread out their wares, oil paintings for pennies, photo postcards, among them a picture of Joseph Stalin surrounded by loving grandchildren. Young beggars, stricken by illness, who do not stop trembling, and their parents nowhere to be seen, and we continue walking, for we have not yet seen the vaulted gate from the fourteenth century. And along its whole length, ancient paving stones, stores and tourists and the sounds of prayer seeping from an open church.—I am going inside the church, I say to my husband, and he remains outside because he is a Jew and he cannot find it in himself to listen to Gentile prayers. And the interior of the church is dim, packed wall to wall with worshippers, and the priest stands there to serve them in their prayers and to direct the singing, and he is a solitary man like my husband. And he speaks of the lack of someone whom he has returned to us, but where is he now? The church is packed, with more people standing than seated, for the space is too small to contain us all. And I stand uneasily among the crowd, for I am not one of the local people and I am not counted among their number. And the

people are listening to the priest's words, and from time
to time they also call out Amen, and I nod my head
with them but do not say Amen, for I am mindful of
my husband waiting outside. When I go out to him, he
asks: How did no evil befall you? For you hurt their
feelings. I answer: Why do you speak to me like that,
my friend, I cannot hurt them in any way. He says: You
went into the church wearing pants. And the words
sink into my heart, and bring me sorrow. I say: No one
looked at me when I came in or when I left, for the
people's attention was on their God. And the light of
the street after the darkness of the church blinds me,
and my eyes fill with tears. And at the end of the street,
a plaza like a market square of bygone days, ringed with
coffee houses, and at the bottom peddlers selling their
wares, wooden objects, spoons and forks and pleasing
chess pieces arranged on wooden boards that could
serve either as box for the chess pieces or the playing
board itself, as you wish, and this was something you
could find anywhere. But some of these are tiny and
others as tall as an average-sized man, as though their
creators are saying: a man's desire to express himself
has no limits, in matters small or large, as a philosopher
by the name of Pascal once said. Indeed, he spoke well,
but he was not exactly precise. For in both small and
large matters, one is hemmed in by restraints, and
human beings are only truly unfettered in their own
thoughts. We sit down in a cafe to rest and my husband
wants to show me more of the wonders and treasures
of Cracow, for he has already toured this city, and he

says: Let's go to the museum after we finish our coffee, but his black mood does not lift as we sit in the cafe. And two women at the cafe order a single cup of tea between them, and take turns drinking from the same cup, thus saving the price of one cup of tea, for in those days the citizens of this country did not have much money. And the two women speak pleasantly to each other, and smile from time to time. I say to myself: If I were like them, I would not feel as heavy-hearted as I do now. And I long for my days as a single woman, when I would meet with girls like me, and with my friend, whom I have not seen for years, I would drink iced coffee from a tall glass, and chase it with a bowl of soft ice cream, for we made this a regular habit in those days. And as we are sitting in the cafe, another couple comes in, and the man and wife sit down at the table next to us, and seem to be dissatisfied about something, and they wordlessly exchange pages of old newspapers which they have brought with them, and their eyes scan the print and their hearts are awake without love. And I said to my husband: See, my friend, what that couple are doing. They are still young, but they are so obviously tired of each other.—Perhaps they have been married for a long time. And my husband fell silent and said nothing more. But two hours later he says: How is your analysis any more impressive than one I have already heard in the past, Madam Architect? Your predecessor was not a doctor and not a nurse, nor was she an architect, one could say, but her analysis differed not a whit from yours. In Jerusalem cafes she would whisper in my ear: Look, those are married, those are not married. She judged according to the looks on their faces. Sonia? I ask,—Yes, Sonia, my husband answers. And I say to myself: What does all this nonsense have to do with me? Let Sonia think what she likes and I will think what I like. And the thought angers me greatly, though I do not understand why.

We stay for some more days in Poland, and the temperatures do not drop. For the country is in the midst of a heat wave, the likes of which have never been seen. And I wonder to myself if this is a sign of the coming destruction of the world, for in those days humankind was seeking signs like that everywhere. And we come to the gallery of Polish painters from the eighteenth and nineteenth centuries, and we wander as the only living souls among the deserted halls, and I say: These paintings are so tiresome, everything is glittering gold and lances and ruins and horsemen and noblemen's castles next to them. How the glory of this country, whose sons are so proud of all these wars, has lost its lustre. And my husband says: Tomorrow we will go all the way to Cracow University, where Copernicus studied before he made his great discoveries, and we'll see what you say then. From the gallery we passed the Wawel castle, with a cathedral beside it, and beyond it the royal cemetery of the Polish kings and queens, from the tenth century all the way to the end of the royal dynasty, and the castle exudes an ancient smell. My husband asks: Should we go in? I say: Let's not go in, because I have already seen this castle from the outside, and its exterior is no different from its interior. My husband asks: How will you know if you don't go inside? I say: It seems to me I will know, and add: It's all the same to me. My husband says: So we won't go in then, and adds: You are so like me.

Now we are at the entrance to Cracow University —a partially paved courtyard, with patches of earth crushed under people's feet, for visitors flock to see where Copernicus the astronomer studied. And even though he was surely only a youth when he studied here, and was only enrolled here for half a year all told, and learned experts have still not managed to find his name in the student rolls beyond the first semester of the second academic year, and after that he is not mentioned again—nevertheless Cracow University is inextricably tied to Copernicus' name, so that his name has become part of the university's name, and his fame which long ago spread beyond Poland's borders has become part of the university's international fame. So we also arrange ourselves in groups, and receive our instructions. The tour of the institution's rooms will be given in three languages, Polish, English and French, so all the visitors must adapt themselves to one of those languages. We join the English-speaking group.

Inside the university, one room leads into another. Where are the hallways? And where did the students walk in Poland's long fall evenings? Where did they ponder in the arcades and halls as they walked? We do not see any of this. We are a group of English speakers, and perhaps we have been found unsuitable to view the place fully. The Polish speakers are shown more, perhaps everything, while our guide—wide in girth and short of stature, bringing to mind a devoted shepherdess of geese—directs her gaze to objects and not places; Here is a clock, with a magnifying glass next to it (designed in the fourteenth century), and here is a lamp engraved with an inscription—*All the peoples in God's light*—and here is a table, an ornamented dean's chair, a cabinet with glass doors, the first of its kind in Europe, here is the student Copernicus' semester certificate with his grades. Nothing special . . . Nothing special . . . Who knows how many unknown Copernicuses studied in this university and have been since lost to the Polish people, so steeped in sorrow were they over their people's fate? A sorrow to which they became addicted, and it came to rule their lives.

The shepherdess leads us from room to room in her own way like a flock of geese, speaking to us along the way in a foreign language, of which I catch only a few words, resolving not to forget those that I estimate will be the most useful to us at some future time. I look around me, and we are in the magnet room now. The magnet was invented in the fifteenth century, the guide tells us. In her right hand she holds a chunk of grey metal, and on the surface of the table metal figures and images move about, pale imitations of the first lights hung in the heavens in the distant past, moving randomly, and it is as if they are trying to enter a long, narrow passageway on which someone has hung a sign reading 'Terra' in Latin. It is an ancient magnetic game. The visitors lean over the table, trying to catch these shapes and images with their hands, hoping perhaps this way to feel something of the magnet's distant force of attraction, but my husband is not among them. Perhaps he hurried away and is now in the innermost room, cut off from the crowd. Perhaps he has found peace of mind.

The last room. Or perhaps it would be more correct to say: the last great hall. Everything flows into here and stops here in the end. Rays of sunlight penetrate the room from below, through tall windows, closed up tight. Sculptures along the walls like Assyrian figures with aristocratic expressions. An ivory stamp. They are Polish kings and their queens. Along one wall, a prayer screen and behind it an altar. Before this, a statue of the holy Queen Jadwiga. Here people stand in contemplation. It is suggested that we bow slightly without moving our feet. We become like shadows in a cave, while the subjects of the kingdom stand eternally, packed closely against each other and against the walls. At the queen's feet is a sign displaying a short biography. Her wonderful life which was also the reason for her death. It happened in the fourteenth century, when the queen was thirty years old. A plague broke out in all of Poland and its territories, which later became known as the Black Thing or the Black Plague. Those who died outnumbered those who survived, for there was no one who recovered once he fell ill, except for a few who lost their beauty in the plague and wanted to die. And Queen Jadwiga, known at that time for her righteousness and for her commanding power which no one had ever refused, put her power to the test, and turned to God with all the strength of her cries on behalf of her people, praying that the plague should cease and the entire Polish people should not be destroyed. And God heard her voice this time, and the plague began to abate, and it was like ebbing floodwaters, slowly receding, but the land was not yet dry. And Queen Jadwiga was infected with the plague while she was walking among the survivors who praised her figure passing among them, and among others who watched her pass without a word, for their bodies were already stricken with the disease. And the queen fell ill and no cure could be found for her, and though God had answered her prayer and halted the plague, He did not have mercy on her life, and she sickened and died. She was the last person to die of the plague in Poland, and with her death the plague came to an end. And what was her shortcoming? Some say that she sinned by sewing herself festive garb on a Sunday, when their religion forbade sewing on Sundays. And what were the garments with which the queen brought this sin upon herself? Shrouds for her approaching wedding with the Saviour, says the guide, and we are already approaching the passageway leading from the great hall out to the courtyard, and while the members of the group are still shaken by the story they have just heard, the guide says: You are free to go wherever you wish, the tour is finished. And suddenly my husband appears at my side, and I do not ask him where were you, and so on, for my heart is still stirred with compassion after the story, and I do not ask my husband if the words have reached his ears too, and I remember the first days of our marriage, when my husband called to me from the second room and said: Come, Naomi, and he spoke the word 'come' in a foreign language, for his thoughts were calmed by the depth of his emotion, and my heart went out to him then.

When we return to the hotel, the owner welcomes us. He tells us that he has run this hotel for the past two years, and that he also serves as the president of the organization of hotels and guest houses in lower Poland. Then he adds: Please forgive me, honoured sir and madam, but your room reservation is through the 14th of this month, and since you have not yet extended your reservation, the room will be turned over to someone else tomorrow. Indeed, we have been negligent, and now we will have to pay the price. Apologies and pleading do not help. We must pack up our bags and leave. The hotel owner looks around him, hoping that perhaps something good will happen, perhaps someone will come to save us, but he cannot help us. So my husband sits with the Cracow telephone book open before him, and he calls hotels and guest houses one after the other until he finds us a place in the restored Jewish quarter Kazimierz, where the local Jews once lived, first voluntarily and later by force. But since the room in Kazimierz will be free only two days hence, we must still find a place to sleep and to shelter in during the day until we can move there. My husband finds us a place at the nunnery at the edge of the city, for one day and one night.

And the pleasant nuns—for thus they are known to everyone—live in a home enclosed by a wall, with a green courtyard filled with various trees, which looks for all the world like a well-maintained public park. But this is the nun's garden, and they care for it to do a good deed and to praise God's wonders, and He also created fruit trees to sate our hunger, while we continue to plant them to thank Him and glorify His name and not to sate ourselves. And the pleasantness of the fruit trees and their fruit shines on the nuns' faces and in all their ways. They have prepared for us a room divided into two areas. One area is for rest and secular conversation, with a table and four chairs and books scattered on the table, and a carpet, and the other area contains two beds next to opposite walls, far from each other. We unpack some of our things and straighten up a little, then go out to take in some fresh air in the garden. As afternoon approaches, the nuns call us by our names, and two of them come to serve us, and we take places in the dining hall with the rest of the nuns, for we are the only guests this day, and we listen to the prayers and blessing after the meal rising from their tables, and one of the nuns ladles out soup for us, and it is potato soup topped with a rubbery milk skin like my mother used to make in my childhood. And the flavour of the soup saturates us and we have never eaten anything so pleasant. And my husband thanks the nuns in their language, for some among them are from my husband's former country, and speak his language, and we have the rest of our meal—vegetables and fruits grown in their garden. We thank them for those too, and all our earlier anger and complaints have melted away, and we have forgotten what brought us here in the first place. A tranquil spirit settles over us. When evening falls, and we lie down to sleep, each of us in our own bed, my husband sits on his bed and recites the prayer before sleep as it is written, and lies down with his face to the wall and falls asleep. He has not come near me since last Tisha b'Av,[36] eight months ago. I say in my heart: My married days are over.

* * *

And from the house of the pleasant nuns we move to the guest house in Kazimierz, for a new day has dawned, and we say farewell to the nuns, notwithstanding our memory of sleeping in the shadow of the cross on their wall, for they have been good to us and we do not hold this against them, and from there we turn our steps towards the old Jewish quarter that was a ghetto before it became once more a Jewish quarter, and there are no Jews left there.

36 'The ninth of the Hebrew month Av', a day on which Jews fast in mourning for the destruction of the Holy Temples in Jerusalem. The First Temple was destroyed by the Babylonians in 587 BCE and the Second Temple was destroyed in 70 CE by the Romans, and Jewish tradition states that both temples were destroyed on the same day in the Jewish calendar, the ninth of Av.

Our days in Kazimierz are few and miserable. Not because the flat made available to us is not pleasant. On the contrary, the flat and indeed the whole building is pleasant, almost new, for the Polish masters are expert at removing the stains of age from buildings and objects, and preserving them like new, and this artistry requires large sums from those hiring their services, and therefore they concentrate on improving the appearance of buildings belonging to the rich and neglect all the rest. Thus the owners of the guest house in Kazimierz have repaired their building as though it was newly built, and they make the upper floor available to us. As I have said, our flat is pleasant, with pleasant appurtenances in the style of the Jews who once lived in this region, such as their closets and beds and clocks and pots in which they cooked their stews, and all their possessions. And the flat faces the main street, the only street, of the quarter. The flat has two rooms, adjacent to each other with no door separating them, and in the language of architects, they form a single space. As an architect, I evaluate each detail on its own merit, and after I have examined all the details, they meld into a single whole, and what I see sinks deep into my soul. I see the whole flat, with my husband in it, like one coming up from the washing.[37]

I say to myself: Naomi, you have followed your husband, where were you actually going? I answer to myself: I have gone wherever he has gone, and set my

37 Echoes Song of Songs 6:6: 'Your teeth are like a flock of sheep coming up from the washing.'

steps according to where he goes. And did you succeed? I go on. No, I did not succeed, I answer myself. And my husband is organizing the flat. What is there to organize? We have been given an orderly flat, but he wants to arrange things according to his wishes. He places his nightclothes on the bed next to the window facing out, and leaves me with the bed in the dimly lit bowels of the room. I accept his division without a fuss. And in my work corner, which I have already set aside in my imagination for writing and reading, made up of a table decorated with mouldings and a cushioned wooden bench next to it—he comes up and says: This will be my rest corner if I am sleepy during the day, here I will sleep during daylight hours and no one will bother me. He goes into the bathroom, takes one of the two large towels placed there for our use, and uses it to wrap the seat cushions on the bench, repeating: This will be my rest place, and goes on: And the second towel too—I will use it to dry myself. And I say nothing, for the saying came to me: I *will not get angry*. He gives me a small hand towel, saying: Use this to dry yourself, and don't move the towel on the bench. I say: As you wish. And to myself I say: The good bed is taken. I have been warned away from the place I had intended to take for myself, and for my bodily needs I have an utterly worthless towel.[38] But I will not get angry. My husband

38 In the Hebrew, the term for 'utterly worthless' is a quote from the Talmud which refers to a document so worthless that its only value was to stop up the mouth of a flask (Talmud, Tractate Baba Kama, 49b).

sees that I do not show any upset, and every morning and evening I shower myself and let the air of the world dry me, and the matter distresses him greatly but he does not utter a word. In his heart he says: She is not trying to restore things to the way they should be. And after the days of our marriage have ended, he will say: You didn't even try.

Three days pass with no change, and on the fourth day my husband goes away for one day to the village of Gorlice, for there his parents left a house and a salt mine which belonged to the grandfather of the family, and my husband has been labouring for years to recover the rights to his family's property which his parents had left behind after they were expelled. He leaves in the morning in order to return that evening, and it is a Thursday. I approach the manager of the guest house, a man of about thirty, benevolent of countenance, and say to him: The matter is thus and such. I would like to get a taxi to the Warsaw airport, if you could possibly help me. One passenger or two? he asks, for he understands immediately, and continues about his business, giving instructions about serving coffee to the table on the right, for they have been waiting a long time. And what about the guests on the balcony, he asks, indicating a youth of about fifteen with one leg missing, still in a wheelchair, with his mother accompanying him, we talked about a veal roast, is that coming along? he asks, and then goes to telephone as he has told me he would.

I wait for him next to the beverage bar. And he: My dear lady, speaking in the Polish way, and perhaps he wanted to say something more but stopped himself, There is a driver. He is fine, his name is Pasha, but he can only do it on Sunday. The fare to Warsaw will be one hundred dollars. I think to myself: One hundred dollars to Warsaw, and one hundred more to move up the date of my airline ticket. I will arrange that when I arrive in Warsaw—it is a small airport. The man shakes my hand to indicate that everything is in order. And don't despair. Thank you, Pan Jacob, I answer in the local vernacular.

In the evening my husband returns, exhilarated. He does not have the patience to tell me everything, but it worked out well. There were arguments during the day, he says, we fought, hard words were spoken, but towards the end of the day—they softened up. In the end we reached an agreement about the house. The salt mine was left for a future discussion. When we parted, we parted with an embrace. My husband is happy. And regarding the salt mine—when we come back here next year, he adds.—We will come . . . I say, Jochanan, I am leaving here. I have already arranged everything. On Sunday a taxi is coming to take me to Warsaw. A driver has been found. My husband understands immediately. Is everything settled? he asks. Perhaps he expected this. And this is what you were doing while I was away? Who recommended the driver?

After that he falls to musing.—It's not that I don't understand, he says finally, but I have one request, he hesitates, Go ahead, but just not on Sunday. Don't cancel your plans, just postpone them. Tell the driver to come on Tuesday instead. I want to show you a few more important things. We have not yet seen the Jewish museum, and we will go to the plaza near here from which the Jews were deported to the concentration camps. Let's talk.—I went by myself to the deportation plaza, I say.

—And . . . ? my husband asks.

—And I am leaving on Sunday.

Two more days, and Sunday morning I awake to find that my whole body is miserable. My eyes are burning while my body is cold and my nose is running. I'm sick! I inform my husband.—You're sick? And you won't cancel your trip?—I am going no matter what, I say, and begin packing various items. I go through the flat—the bathroom, the work corner which my husband turned into his rest place, the Jewish clothes closet, bookcase, ornamented buffet, the decorated table with the bowed legs, bed, another bookcase, my gaze brushes all these, and I scoop up the last of my possessions, passing over anything that is his. The taxi arrives but does not honk. Pasha the driver waits politely. The director of the guest house also accompanies me. My husband is embarrassed in their presence. There are no more words between us, but my heart is singing: I am going to Warsaw. And where is Warsaw?

Warsaw is a two-hour taxi ride away. Two? Maybe five?
Five hours to be precise . . . And let it be seven, I add
another line to my song, and let it be fifty, let it be forty,
I am going to Warsaw from here. I climb into the back
seat of the taxi, and my husband is outside the taxi,
stroking my wrist through the window.

I remember: We travelled on the Cracow tram
from one end of the city to the other, and my husband
was explaining to me about streetcar fares in Poland.
Here, he says, instead of paying the driver, you insert
coins into the slit in the pole. I looked around me.
Indeed, there were metal poles on each side of the car,
and a slit down the middle of each one.—And don't
even think of not paying, as if you could avoid it easily,
as if there is no one supervising, my husband continues, perhaps there is an inspector and perhaps there
isn't, but don't you get caught. You would have to pay a
fine equal to half your annual salary, it's not worth the
risk. And I asked: Why should I get caught? I'm not
someone who tries to avoid paying. So I won't get
caught. And my husband again: Anything is possible,
look, I've warned you . . . Perhaps you will travel alone
once . . . It is not the practice in this place.[39] We were
travelling to Kazimierz then, and an insect stung my
wrist. Later I found out that it was known to the locals
as 'the boxcar insect'. My hand swelled up, and when

39 Echoes Genesis 29:26: 'But Laban responded, "It's not the
practice of our place to give the younger one in marriage before
the firstborn."'

we got out on the pavement, stepping over the gap between the car and the steep incline of the street, my hand was burning like fire. Jochanan! You're a doctor! I called for help. And he, as a knowledgeable expert, was not particularly impressed. You deserve the sting and the sting deserves you, he joked, looking at my hand from a distance without moving a muscle to save me. And unlike then, when he did not come close to touch my hand but just looked at it from a distance with the eye of an expert, now he looks at my wrist up close and holds it tightly like someone who knows nothing of medicine and is not an expert in anything but is becoming more lost by the minute. And unlike when we got out of the tram and he looked at the wound on my hand from afar, without sympathy, now he tries to find my palm and bring it to his face like someone who has lost everything and hopes to find it anew within my palm. And suddenly the young guest-house manager returns with a colourful scarf around his neck, as though he too has fallen ill and needs to protect himself from changes in climate, and he has a package in his hands, wrapped in brown paper. Take this, he urges, I brought you a peasant's jar. One more small thing for your luggage. A souvenir from us.

Now it is just me and Pasha the driver. Polish songs about cavalrymen and their lovers on his tape deck, and a woman with a cold in the back seat. When will we get there? In five or four hours? To catch a cold in the middle of the summer. Strange. Dear Pasha, on the way will we stop to rest at a roadside cafe? What was all this? A woman who does not know where she is going, does not forget where she has been, and where was the beauty? Where did tree branches bend down to catch a few words from the streams of voices passing beneath them? I was an architect and I did not know how to create beauty, the Polish builders did not teach me everything they knew, did not teach me the secret of returning.

I remember more: It was in the first days of my marriage, and I was in our house, taking a shower in lukewarm water. My husband came in. In his hands a large towel like an open hand, wide, and he wrapped me in it and he too was clean like one coming up from the washing. And I was wet. Thus only I was wrapped in a towel, and he was the one who wrapped me. I said: I will dry myself. And he said: No, let me do it. And we walked to the room step by step, and it was as though he supported my steps lest I slip from his hands, lest my skin dry off in the air of the room without him, and how pleasant his touch was to me then. And the driver Pasha says: if Madam would like to rest, you can lean back here ... I see that Madam has caught an illness in our Poland ... —No, it's nothing, Pasha. It's just a head cold which will be gone in a week, remembering an old joke: If we treat it properly, it will pass within seven days. Pasha says, Here we say: Maybe she ate something bad ... about everything we say: Maybe he ate something bad ... For example, our president took a bribe?

Maybe he ate something bad . . . Pasha joked. His own old joke. And I see before my eyes: A small towel. Scarcely big enough to seal up the mouth of a little bottle. And I said . . . My husband is next to me, like the palm of a hand he spreads his arms towards his baby girl. And though that time he did not leave me an inch of wet skin that was not dried, and a single towel covered the whole world and protected me, now he turns to me with a tiny scrap of fabric that cannot absorb anything and says: This is your towel. God has made me laugh.[40] I lean into the back seat of the car and close my eyes. And once when we travelled outside the city, we came to an estate with streams in the midst of a forest. We rented ourselves a room for a day, a night, and another day, and they prepared a meal in our honour. And outside were black swans in a pool.—The pool is ours, and the swans are ours, and the forest is ours, the estate owners said, Thanks be to God who cleansed Poland of unwanted creatures for us. We did not know of whom they spoke, and did not ask. That night, I woke with intense cramps. The hosts had indeed prepared a feast for us, including oily meat dumplings. And I did not curb my appetite and ate something that was bad for me, for the trip through the forest had made me hungry. I was beset by nausea, and I could neither vomit to relieve myself nor calm down. And my husband, the doctor, saw that my face was pale

40 Genesis 21:6: 'Sarah said, "God has made me laugh. Everyone who hears will laugh with me."'

and spasms were wracking my body, and he got up quickly from his bed and went first to the three tall windows in the room and pulled the cords of the blinds to open the windows wide. And clean night air entered the room but did not help me, and he brought me water to drink and that did not help me, and he brought me to the sink, and placed his palm on my forehead and rubbed it, and I leant against him and felt a little better. And I went back to my bed like one blinded, groping in the dark, and my husband went back to his bed next to the windows and said nothing more, good or bad. The air in the room was cool and good, and my husband did not close the windows. I remained awake in my bed until almost morning, finally falling asleep about an hour before dawn.

PART THREE

Divorce and What Follows

Pasha brought me in his car all the way to the airport. The tape of Polish songs had fallen silent. Pasha grew serious. Now he had to return to Cracow, and it was almost evening. I paid his fare and added a tip. We parted as friends for the moment. Farewell Poland. A small airport, two storeys. On the first floor—Security. Luggage. Check-in. On the second floor—clocks on the walls. Four medium-sized stores: Watches. Snacks and wines. Perfumes and all kinds of soaps. Shirts. Newspapers. Cheap jewellery. More perfumes, more clocks on the walls. Their steady ticking was like a cause for celebration. I will not wait here for a year. Not a week and not a month but, rather, an hour, an hour and a half I will wait, and the mobile steps will be pulled up to the aeroplane, we will climb the steps to the heavens. A band of travellers are returning home, to Holon, teenaged travellers entering the watch store and I join them.—Counsellor! Can I buy a watch?

Counsellor, what do we do with leftover zlotys? What an experience that Auschwitz was . . . and I am among them. Their company pleases me and here I am with them, I am travelling to Holon. Holon which is in Israel. Israel which is in Jerusalem. Jerusalem which is in Tel Aviv. I buy a Polish watch to hang as a souvenir around my neck. What beautiful music, the melody of this watch. The watch's symphony. Behold how good and how pleasant, whines a sick person who has just recovered. I have recovered but I am not healthy. I am not healthy because I was ill and the illness stayed in me. The illness is sleeping and even if we guard its sleep carefully we can do no more than scare it.

Other days arrived. Accompanied by my brother and his wife, I travelled to my husband's flat in Jerusalem while my husband was still in Poland. On the way to his house, while we were still on the path bypassing the building where Old Shapira lived, I did not see the boy with the crippled leg any more. And daylight was fading away, and an obstacle was in my way, and I did not see it and tripped and fell, and my brother and his wife shouted: Get up right away! If something knocks you down, you shouldn't stay there. And I absorbed the blow I had received and recovered and got up, but from then on I limped on my knee. And I opened the door to my husband's flat with the key he had entrusted to me long ago, and now I was using it for the last time, and I said to myself, this word 'use', it too has been infected with some kind of illness.

And I unlocked the door and went in, opening the suitcase I had brought with me. Into it I stuffed the remaining books which had been my companions up to now and the music tapes, filled with pleasant and pained voices, and I took my folded clothes and the ones hanging in the closet, and from the closet I took out shoes and one winter outfit, and I said in my heart: I will not be like that Sonia, the former doctor whose clothes claimed her territory in this flat and did not relinquish the place that was originally designated for them. Whereas she disappeared and slipped away from him. And we collected the clothes and books and notebooks, and turned to leave, and I said to my family: Wait a little and I will go say farewell to the Eybeschutz family, for we ate at their table three or four times on a Sabbath evening since I arrived here, when they were contemplating the questions of the Land of Israel and the Western Wall and our right to all the settlements. And my brother said: Go ahead up and we will wait. And they took the things we had packed and brought them to the car in which we had come.

The Eybeschutz family generally went to sleep late in the evening. And they would run between the rooms of their flat as though on wheels, moving furniture from its place in preparation for the few hours of sleep left to them, and my husband and I would lie in our bed and listen to the sound, and my husband would say: They are active when everything around is still, and I did not know if he was saying this as condemnation or praise, for their flat was built above ours and we heard the sounds of their footsteps every night. I knocked on their door, for I knew that they would not be asleep at this hour, and Israel Eybeschutz opened the door and said: You are already back? Welcome! I told them how things stood, for his wife Miriam, having finished dragging her bed and her husband's bed into place, had joined us, and I went on to say that we had not returned together, but that Jochanan had stayed alone on Polish soil, as had been planned, and had not cut his trip short as I had. Well . . . said Israel. Well, we are separating. I came to say thank you, I will not forget you. And Israel Eybeschutz's wife reached out and hugged me briefly, and Israel also reached out and embraced me wordlessly. And I sobbed for a long time into his shoulder and the side of his neck without knowing why, and could not be comforted. And Israel and his wife soothed me: There, there, that's enough . . . And my family was waiting for me by the car which had brought us here, and I still refused to be comforted and words just added to my sorrow. And the springs of my tears burst forth and Israel's arm hugged me because I clung to it as I wept, for I regretted that I had left my husband, left Jochanan, in a foreign country, and he was not with me.

Bitter days followed, different from all the ones which had come before. Tears filled my eyes whenever someone threatened to pronounce the word 'Jochanan' in my hearing. I could not even hear the name 'Chanan' without tears, for it reminded me of a similar name. And we still did not cease speaking to each other in our thoughts, and we sent our voices to each other through our telephones. Even so we did not cease preparing, each of us with an advisor at our side, what was required for a divorce decree. And there was no real difficulty in this, for there were no claims between us, and what did come up could not be formulated in legal language, and I said to myself: Go out and see people going about their daily work and it will be good for you, and they are clean and washed and they have changed their clothes after the night's sleep and sprayed their bodies with perfume, and I saw all these as heroes, worthy of praise. I said to myself: I wish I were like them. And I came to my husband's place to sign a detailed agreement between us which paved the way for the divorce decree. And I said to him: It would be good to meet in a cafe. I suggested Cafe Nitzan, where we once sat next to a group of women, psychologists from Jerusalem, who were discussing their patients' dreams and hid nothing from one another or those around them, other customers, and my husband did not believe in psychologists then, and was happy that I also did not approve of them. And he said: I can understand you, it was also difficult for me to sit at home on the day when I returned from Poland and you were not there, and your clothes and all your possessions were taken away, and that night I went to sleep at the nearby Shlisel Hotel. And we were like two friends who meet again after a long time, speaking in a language that no one sitting near them understands, but they understand, and we were like two clerks who earn their living working for an accountant, like two day labourers who are barely scraping by and they strengthen one another with their words. And I asked my husband: How much did you earn then? And he said: I earned enough to buy you a closet with two doors, for your clothes, with room in it for shoes as is the custom of Asiatic people. He said 'Asiatic people' but he meant a condemnation of the locals. I was silent. And I looked troubled.[41] Each of us drank two steaming cups of coffee and my husband did not get angry when I spelt out for the young waitress my request for the correct proportions of ingredients in the coffee. And it should be hot, I added, and my husband did not get angry as he usually did, and his expression did not lose its tranquillity, and it was as if he said: I am not the one fated to live next to this spoilt woman and spend my days beside one for whom the demands of her body take precedence over all else, and it is not my task to change her personality and her ways. And we both signed the agreement, and my husband promised me that tomorrow he would give the signed papers to his lawyer, and he, who has ties to people in the Rabbinate, would expedite the divorce decree. And just as my husband once burnt to arrange our marriage as quickly as possible, even as early as the week of Passover,

41 The language in Hebrew echoes Genesis 40:6: 'When Joseph came to them in the morning, he saw that they were troubled.'

and went every day to the old Rabbinate building in Jerusalem and hounded the Sephardic chief rabbi and the Ashkenazi chief rabbi and their deputies, pressing them to act on our behalf, for he lacked the necessary confirmation of his personal status, having immigrated from a foreign country, and he stood over them to speed the process along, so he laboured now to expedite the divorce decree and pushed his lawyer, and the rabbinical counsellor whom he had hired for himself in one of the corridors of the Rabbinate, to finish everything before the court adjourned for its holiday break which would last three months and three days. And we signed the preliminary agreement and I returned to my house in Tel Aviv on a bus that left from the Central Bus Station.

—Again I watch my shadow, my husband is speaking to me on the telephone just like he did before our marriage, and I see it creep onto the opposite pavement and onto the stone wall of the building opposite us, for the day is coming to an end after the evening prayer and I return home and the shadow is still wandering on the stone face of the building, made of pale stones like other Jerusalem buildings, and from there it rises to the roofs of the neighbours' houses and continues upwards, and it seems to me that it has disappeared, for there are no chimneys in Jerusalem . . . My husband jokes a little, and I understand that the divorce decree is approaching completion and that my husband's advisors and lawyer have brought their work to a successful conclusion.

And my husband paid two more visits to the 'Office of the Eight Lawyers', whose director had become his lawyer. Writing up the agreement did not pose any particular difficulties, and I did not make a fuss over occasional changes he wanted to make, as various apprehensions assailed him, but he was not satisfied until new delays occurred. Once, when he was already turning to leave for home after spending an extended amount of time at the 'Office of the Eight', for he had established himself with the office staff as a demanding client, and they could not imagine receiving him without detaining him there, and they would put him off with various claims, and my husband did not understand what they were doing and just complained about these delays, as though they stemmed from the lawyers' negligence, he was on his way home, carrying the final documents, glancing over them from time to time as he walked, and while he was striding along King George Street, on the exposed section of the street, he passed the Chatam Sofer's small shop, and to his left a public park open to the elements, through which blew a city wind, which snatched the pages of the agreement from his hands, carrying them towards the park. The park in question slopes down from King George Street towards Damascus Gate, which runs parallel to it, and it is all steps and curving rocks with thorny flower bushes between them, and my husband's gaze followed the pages as they drifted down the slope, finally burying themselves in the dust of one of the small limestone rises which were brought to the

park when its architects once decided to give it a
facelift. And in his heart, my husband gave up on the
documents and thought, Well, it is not as though the
documents are such a valuable find, it's not a love letter
from the monk Abelard to his beloved, it is a letter
from a lawyer. I will just go and get another copy.

Two days later, my husband retraced his steps, and
waited an hour or two in the same reception room of
the 'Office of the Eight'. When his turn came, he saw
to his business and set out for home again, agreement
in hand. And when he passed by King George Park and
his eyes lit on the beautiful foliage he could see from
outside the park, he eased his grip on the pages slightly
before he caught himself, and the pages escaped his
hands a second time and began rolling before him
like a pack of white dogs, for they had come unstapled
and flew in all directions, and my husband chased
them like a man battling his destiny fearlessly, without
heeding the goddesses of fate. He continued chasing
the runaway pages until he caught two of them and
then returned home, giving up on the remaining three.
He called the office of the eight lawyers and requested
a new copy of the entire agreement.—And please send
it by registered mail to my official post-office box, he
said. All these things he recounted to me by telephone
because they seemed wondrous to him, and I laughed
and said: Write these things down, for it sounds like
they belong in a novel, and the lawyer presented the
signed agreement to the rabbinical advisor, and the

rabbinical advisor passed it on to the head of the court, for the two were related by marriage, and the divorce decree began wending its way through the halls of the rabbinical court, and the date of the divorce was set for the 11th of Elul[42] of that year.

The day of the divorce arrived, and it was like all days which come to an end eventually. And I dressed in my most becoming outfit for I mused to myself, perhaps my husband will notice how nice I look and reconsider the divorce and he will call out to the judges sitting on the court, Stop, and will ask for my hand in marriage a second time, and I will say: But we are already married, Jochanan. And I took a taxi to Jerusalem. The courtroom was full of people. And thus it will always be in that room, that new doors will always swing open on their hinges, as some people come in and others go out, and it will always be the way of the world that people seek happiness and truth and strive to distance themselves from suffering and despair, but neither of those can be found. And the rabbinical advisor hovered about us and did not leave us alone, reminding me of beggars I had seen in the cemetery. Is he waiting for a tip, and will he wax fat with our suffering? The advisor bowed with an actor's theatrical bow and said: Mr and Mrs Tobias are called to the judges' chambers. And the door to the room was inscribed with the word *Divorces*.

42 The last month of the Jewish year, in late summer or early autumn.

I remember very little. Five judges sat behind a narrow table, dressed in their usual colours, black and white, and one was almost a lad, whose beard was no more than the pale down of a miniature bird. He must be a genius, I thought, if they have seated him among these learned, elderly judges, when he is so much younger. He could have been their grandson. They asked our names, and we answered. I stated my name and my husband stated his. They asked my husband whether he had ever been called by a nickname. My husband responded: My mother called me Chanan-che and my old teacher called me Choni the Circle Drawer.[43] The judges wrote down his words without cracking a smile. And my husband added: The Christian students in the university called me Alexander.—Alexander? asked the most elderly judge in amazement, and the rest of the judges also wrote down 'Alexander' in amazement, and my husband added in an even tone, as if it were all the same to him: And sometimes Alex. The judges wrote down 'Alex'. And did you have no other name? the young judge suddenly asked, for he was curious and perhaps he knew something more. Another name? my husband thought for a moment. Some people in synagogue call me Nachman. The neighbour from the third floor calls me Rabbi Jochanan.—And by what name are you

43 A Jewish sage of the first century BCE, described in the Talmud as a miracle worker who brought rain during a drought by drawing a circle, standing in it and telling God that he would not move until it rained.

called to the Torah? asked the young genius.—When I am called to the Torah, they say: Rabbi Jochanan Tobias son of Mordechai and Esther from the Saklovski family. That's enough for now, said the senior judge, and studied the list before him for some time. Then I was called to the judges' bench, where they placed some object in my hand, I do not remember what, and instructed me to walk with this foreign object in my hand, all the way to the window at the back of the room, touch the window with one hand and then retrace my steps and return the object to the judges' bench. Thus I set out. But when I reached the window it opened at my touch. And I understood that not all the women who carried out this ritual actually returned the object to the judges' bench, for the window showed them what was below it, and there a chasm yawned. I remembered my long-time friend who answered the window's call by throwing herself on it, and I returned to the judges' bench with the object in my hand, and on my head was a veil which was the opposite of a bride's wedding veil. And I recalled the words of my husband's friend who came from Akko to our wedding, who spoke of dust on our wedding day, even though he said both pearls and dust. And the senior judge spoke: You are hereby permitted to any man. And my husband repeated these words like an echo from far-off days. And we left the judges' room, that is, the divorce room, and entered the lift together. We descended the five or six floors to the street level, and my husband hugged me all the way down.

And more days passed, which seemed to me end-less, though for those around me they were only a few days, and I resumed some of my former pursuits, and others I did not resume. And my former manager, Mr Davidov, who had heard the story of our marriage from beginning to end, asked about me. Mr Davidov is asking after you, said my neighbour from the next building, for she had somehow also heard the details of my story. I called Mr Davidov, and he said to me: Welcome back to us. A position is opening up in our office. Even though the position is for a receptionist and not an architect, come back to us. I think being with people will be good for you. Come be with us for a while. I thanked him in my heart, and out loud I said: I'll think about it, my friend, and get back to you. At that time a rumour reached me: Your former husband, they said, had an operation on one of his kidneys and is lying in Sha'arei Tzedek Hospital in Jerusalem, go visit him. And I wondered what had happened, for my husband was in the habit of calling me from time to time, and had not mentioned kidney disease, and instead told me of the time he was wandering through the Four Species market to choose himself a suitable citron fruit for the coming holiday, having already pur-chased the other three species earlier in the day and placed them on his porch, wrapped in a damp towel like the rolled-up Persian rugs placed on top of one of his closets, and my husband would moisten them every six or seven hours so they would not dry out. And while he was walking through this market, it seemed to him that laughing eyes were peeking at him from among the palm branches, which were placed diagonally, leaning against one another, like a temporary fence, and people would come up and feel them, and that is why my husband hurried to buy the other species earlier in the day, so that people would not touch them so much, for my husband did not like the touch of people's hands and also avoided the touch of lips, for their presence aroused in him a certain disgust. And my husband approached the palm-branch fence, to view it from up close, and noticed the laughing face of an innocent-looking youth, and recognized the genius youth who had presided on our court and interrogated him about his name, and now he was laughing at him and my husband did not understand why, and he decided to ask him something. But the genius youth disappeared from his sight. And my husband turned this way and that, and went to the willows section and dug through their dust, and there was nothing there, and then went to look among the myrtle boughs that were inserted between branches of green bushes, jutting out towards passers-by as if they had always grown there. And the myrtle gave off a sweet fragrance, and my husband saw beyond it the youth backing away, no longer smiling but sad and distant as though his time in this world had come to an end and he had to hurry. And my husband pursued him for a few moments and even called several times: Sir! Sir! For he had never found out his name and did not know how he was called in public, since he was a great genius in Torah.

But the youth broke into a run, and my husband, who was not athletic, ran after him briefly and then gave up and went on his way, and all these things he told me in detail as he held the telephone receiver in his house in Jerusalem, and did not say a word about his illness.

* * *

And I travelled to the city of Jerusalem to see how my husband was doing, for he had undergone surgery on one of his kidneys. I was told that his suffering had already eased and that he was doing well, and I came to the hospital, which was located in the centre of town, and I remembered how we walked there to buy cheese pastries for Sarah the cleaning lady, and shampoo for my husband's hair, and meanwhile I passed open hospital wards, separate for men and women, and pictures of nurses, like airline stewardesses, hanging on the walls all around, instructing: 'Quiet. This is a hospital.' I remembered my childhood, and I thought, Where do those pictures come from? I asked the nurse at the desk whether I was in the kidney ward, and she answered: Yes. I asked: Is there a patient here by the name of Dr Jochanan Tobias? She riffled through some papers and answered: Yes, there is.—Where can I find this patient? The nurse indicated a room with a wide doorway at the end of the corridor. I approached the entrance to the room and then drew a bit closer. I was still a stone's throw away when I first caught sight of him. He lay by the window as he loved to do, with his bed in the shadow of the window where the light came through—and at that moment my husband saw me and lifted one hand in greeting, and a strange woman sat on his bed whom I did not know. And I chose not to come any closer, but my husband called: Come, Naomi, as he had called me in the past, in another language, and he extended his raised hand towards me. And his hand protruded from the bedframe towards me, and I looked at it and backed away without a word. I returned to the corridor, and went back by the nurse sitting behind the counter and the other nurse in the photograph which read: 'Quiet. This is a hospital' with her finger to her lips as a sign, and I went down the stairs without taking the lift and my husband's hand still hovered before me, though I did not know why. For it was really a matter of no importance whatsoever.

The street was flooded with sunlight. Winter had not yet arrived and the autumn sun brought with it green flies just as it had brought them the previous autumn. And I thought about the joy of children riding on a carousel on horses of wood and metal, and how someone once dreamt of setting up a carousel at every beach and in every country, for any adult who experiences one in his childhood will think twice before rushing out to battle or defining any battle in which he fights as a defence of the homeland, since in his childhood he experienced things which contain truth and beauty. And for a moment I wondered whether the cafe in Jerusalem still existed, where my aunt took me when I was a child, when she ordered me a tall glass of iced chocolate with ice cream and whipped cream, while I was looking at pictures in magazines, and I still remembered the name of the cafe: 'Good Taste'. But there was no point in searching for it. I would look ridiculous. And I said: I will go visit the Academy of the Immortals before I leave Jerusalem.

The Academy is located near the president's house, and it is an Academy for immortals because those accepted within its gates are guests forever, not merely temporarily, even if it is not entirely clear that this is their place. And the Academy is built high on a hill, though the building itself is not tall. It is wide, however, occupying a large tract of land, with round columns in the front as is the custom of wealthy aristocrats who thus appoint their homes, and the columns hold up a roof with doves' wings on both sides, looking to me like the Greek Parthenon, and the steps leading up to it are white as marble. I climbed the steps and it seemed to me that I became part of the vast crowd who were exiled and insisted on coming back again to see the pavement made of sapphire, as clear as the sky, but the second time too they were exiled, for they were great in number, and that time they were exiled forever. And the immortals who have been accepted to the academy sit in the rooms of the building, each man in his own room, and the rooms have been given to them permanently and perhaps even longer. And they lean over a large desk, with books and bags piled up before them. And their hair is long and white, and

some exhibit wild beards. And they number a few
women among them, some with noticeable beards like
a woman I once saw in the corridor of the Bank of
Israel, typing with her face to the wall. And in the corridor hang portraits of all who those who have been
accepted to this place, displayed in a straight line, one
after another, and the portraits are so similar to one
another that there is little to distinguish between them.
And next to each portrait an engraved metal plate bears
the name of its subject, and a map instructs the viewer:
You are here now. And this is how to find the immortal
one whose location is indicated by his portrait. And
once in a great while, every seventy or eighty years, a
new immortal joins the existing ones and space is
made for him among his colleagues. And I said to
myself: I will go and visit the greatest physicist of the
generation, who lives in this building, and I will hear
from him about the fate of the world. And I went up to
the wall of portraits and honed in on the image of
Professor Jacob Lestschinsky, whose name was praised
by everyone even in my childhood, and whose fame
continues to spread. I had no difficulty understanding
the map's instructions, for I was used to reading maps,
and the immortal Lestschinsky was poring over his
books and maps that very hour, and I knocked on the
door of his room and went in, and he looked up at me
in surprise: What could a young maiden want from old
fogeys like us?—I am not a young maiden, I protested,
and I did not know if that was a compliment on the
scientist's part or an attempt to create reality with his

words. I saw that before my arrival he had been poring over a map of the world as viewed by people in the first centuries of our era: the Mediterranean Sea in the centre, North Africa in the middle, all the Mediterranean countries to the north of it, and all of them forming a stylized ellipse.—I came to ask about the world, sir, if you would be so kind as to tell me, what is the world? And moreover, were the early Greeks correct when they said that everything that has been created must end? And the scholar said: I have also heard thus. Then he looked at me and went on: Come closer and I will show you the map of Herodotus the Great. And I came closer to him and thought, perhaps he will say something that I will keep in my heart. And his body exuded a smell of stale urine while his eyes burnt with a strange fire, and he said: The same Herodotus who died before his time . . . The same Herodotus who was invited to the palace of the King of Macedon, and who was an excellent cartographer . . . —Cartographer? I asked, I thought he was an historian of ancient times.—Of course of ancient times, the scholar said, he lived his life in ancient times . . . I considered his words briefly.—Your words sound strange to me, I finally said.—Strange . . . The scholar repeated my words reflectively. It's possible they are strange . . . Look, for instance, how heated I am. Come close for a moment, my child, why did you move so far away, I can barely see you, touch my forehead, how I am burning now, and again the scholar's eyes burned and it was as if he were speaking obscenities into his beard.

I was like someone caught in a maze. I found my way out only by walking along the walls, touching the wall until it led me to the door. I put my hand on the door handle and pushed the door outward. I did not call out but only opened it towards other comers, but no other comers arrived, and I slipped out of the door to the corridor and sped all the way to the main gate of the Parthenon, and the white steps appeared, like ice, and a living fence of immortal bushes and flowers. I passed all these by. And unlike my husband, who lengthened his stride until he was running, while we were on our way to the bus stop going to the hospital, like someone running away from something, I also picked up my pace now until I was running, but to get closer to something instead. I ran straight into the street, where there were police cars parked next to the president's house. A uniformed officer stopped me, rather apologetically, and a blue light rotated noisily above us. Where are you running around to? 'Running around' he said, not 'running', and I did not protest.— To a friend's, I said.—And what is his name? the police officer inquired, perhaps in jest.—What is his name .. . I respond, when I see him I will ask his name.

I ran to the old leper colony, and a kind of new song moved within me: Today . . . Today . . . The police officer was still waving at me as if to say: Don't I have enough crazy people to deal with? But who is the crazy one here, for someone once said to me: I will wait all day for your coming.

I had not been here for a long time. In the court-yard—brambles. No cultivated garden flowers here. Three fruit trees bent their branches low. One with inedible fruit, the second and third with edible fruit. Next to the entrance were old tires with bicycles leaning against them. This was the only new thing that had been introduced there since I last saw it. There was no cripple and no blind person and all their diseases had been healed. Naomi, I said to myself, why did you continue to remember them, the cripples and the blind, those stricken with boils, and I said: Here I am.

And a human hand swung open both halves of the door. The man said: Come in, I have been waiting for you. And he said to me: You finally made it here, or some similar words. I cannot remember for sure. We went into the building where the man had fixed himself up a simple hut to live in. It seemed to me that it lacked for nothing, for the wooden walls were well sealed and gave off a pleasant fragrance. He lacked for nothing. I remembered that on my way here I had passed a news-stand at which I used to stop for a look whenever I passed that way, at the top of the road, with my husband by my side. And the news seller used to spread out his newspapers for all passers-by, so that they would learn what is new in the world since yesterday, awakening a desire to know more, and they would buy his newspapers. And when I passed by today, I saw that the news-stand owner no longer spread his newspapers outside the booth, and instead had brought them inside and covered them with opaque wrappers so that passers-by would not peek at them and satisfy their curiosity without paying, thus decreasing his sales. And he said in his heart: They will become curious if they do not know a thing, and they will pay for the knowledge. And the news-stand owner has slept well ever since, for he has ceased giving things away for free and thus his mind is more at peace, and even though his profits have decreased, he has remained tranquil. I passed by the news-stand and took the change to heart.

Chanan, for such was the name of the guard who watched over the old leper colony, said, I never told you my name, though I heard your husband speak your name when you passed by here, my name is Chanan. I said: How that is like . . . Chanan asked: Like what? I said: Like the name of the one who once accompanied me here, but we will not speak of that any more. And now the two of us were inside the same house which I used to see from the outside when I passed along the way, but now I was seeing it from within. And it seemed to me that those two images had nothing in common with each other. I told Chanan that I saw light coming from these rooms last Passover eve when I passed with my husband on our way to the Seder meal, and I looked and saw a faint light in the window. Did you celebrate Passover alone? I asked Chanan and he smiled and did not answer. Then he said: Your image came to me then. Chanan recounted for me the history of this leper colony, which he had been assigned to guard years ago. He added that the building was not empty and neglected now for most of the patients had returned here when they were no longer ill, for they could not find themselves a place in the world, and now each one was busy with his own affairs.—They do not demand anything of me, he said.—But you live among them, I said.—Yes, he answered. As for me, I take on a few responsibilities even if they no longer ask it of me, such as keeping the place clean and tidy, and repairs which I continue to make, and just an hour before you arrived, I towed away two full bins of brambles and dry hawthorn branches from the plants that grow wild here.

—And the others, what do they say? I asked.

—The others—every man for himself.

—They are not too old for that? I asked Chanan.

—No . . . Here one does not grow old, you will see.

In the evenings he would ride his bicycle. Sometimes he would get as far as the centre of town and he would return with his bicycle basket laden with various small objects, to make me happy. And once we joined a sightseeing tour, to see the Dead Sea before all its waters dried up and disappeared. In the mornings we would hear the sounds of water bubbling in the pool which had been here forever, planned by the original architect to be on a slight slope, so that water flowed into it from the Siloam Spring. And Chanan entered the house, and when he came back—behold! In his hands he held two cups of steaming coffee on a single tray.

End of Naomi's Words